WOMEN IN LUST

WOMEN IN LUST

WOMEN IN LUST
EROTIC STORIES

EDITED BY
RACHEL KRAMER BUSSEL

CLEiS
PRESS

Published in the United States by Cleis Press, Inc., 2246 Sixth Street, Berkeley, California 94710.

Printed in the United States.
Cover design: Scott Idleman/Blink
Cover photograph: Jonathan Storey/Getty Images
Text design: Frank Wiedemann

First Edition.
10 9 8 7 6 5 4 3 2 1

Trade paper ISBN: 978-1-57344-724-9
E-book ISBN: 978-1-757344-744-7

Contents

INTRODUCTION: LADIES WHO LUST

Lust. It's one of those four-letter words that trips off the tongue. When I say it out loud, it makes my lips want to curve into a smile. Lust is more than simple arousal; it is the force that makes us not just turned on, but craving a certain person (or people).

I used to write a sex column called "Lusty Lady," named after the famed strip club, but somehow *lusty,* rhyming as it does with busty, sounds a bit like a joke, an added bit of humor, which is how our culture often treats sex. *Lust,* though, is different; it's intense, overpowering. While in real life we may not always act every time lust calls to us, in fiction, we can abandon the safety of propriety and seek out lust and sex wherever we find them.

The characters in *Women in Lust* may vary in the objects of their lust, and how they go about acting on their urge, but what connects them is that pure impulse for a lover. Sometimes he is someone she knows well, is married to or dating; in other stories, he is a stranger, and is sexy precisely because he represents the unknown. Women also lust after other women here, as in Kayar Silkenvoice's Japanese happy ending massage story, "Cherry Blossom," and while we only hear one side of the story, I'd like to think the working woman is doing more than just her job. In addition to the culture clash, there's the joy of throwing caution to the wind while on vacation, using travel to broaden one's sexual horizons. Whether watching a lover playing guitar, using a webcam, going out for a smoke or simply embracing a chance encounter, these women seize the opportunities presented to them, and savor the lovers who teach them about themselves and help them open up to new sensual possibilities. Sometimes that means looking at the man they live with in a new light, and other times that means something much naughtier. Either way, their lust is a valued part of their lives, not a pesky afterthought or to-do list item on "date night."

The objects of their lust are not always the "right" person. In "Rain," a woman falls for her best friend's boyfriend, one of the ultimate dating taboos, but she goes for it. Sometimes the desire itself, the way it can be used to tease and taunt, as in Charlotte Stein's "Guess," is maddening, but we embrace our lusts even when they are maddening, even when they make us do things we might otherwise consider reckless.

For every woman here who can locate her lust on the map of her body, who zeros in on her target and goes for it, there is another who is opened up to her lust by a lover, such as Jen Cross's narrator pondering what it was, exactly, her orally generous long-ago lover got out of being between her legs. The first words of Shanna Germain's powerfully kinky "Beneath My Skin" are "I'm afraid," to which her lover, Kade, responds, "You should be." Fear can be a powerful motivator and, crossed with lust, can lead to explosive results.

Whether discovering the joy of a younger man, not to mention some delicious pudding, in "Comfort Food," by Donna George Storey, or taking sex and bondage into the great outdoors in "Something to Ruin" by Amelia Thornton, these women indulge in new ways of getting off and pushing the limits of their lust. Thornton writes: "Despite my longing, there was still part of me that wanted to protest, to tell him to cut me loose, to run wildly through the forest back to the safety of our picnic blanket, but to me that is the beauty of rope: to desire escape but to willingly be imprisoned, to feel the pressure of something that prevents my movement, yet to know there is no place that I feel safer than when trapped like this." She captures the excitement of giving in to a dominant lover, even when there is a small part of the narrator that is unsure, for that is precisely the part that fuels her desire. This story captures the true power that lies in submission and the many joys it can bring. In "Her, Him, and Them," by Aimee Pearl, the narrator submits to various lovers who question her and push her not only to be the best sub she can be, but to figure out why, exactly, she likes the thrill of submission and service.

I hope these stories inspire some lusty days and nights for you, as they have for me.

Rachel Kramer Bussel
New York City

NAUGHTY
THOUGHTS

Portia Da Costa

Are you having those naughty thoughts again, you bad girl? I can always tell, because your eyes start to cross."

Terrence accompanies his accusation with a swirl of his hips, a move that nearly blows the top of my head off. It also nearly dislodges said naughty thoughts he's accusing me of, but not quite. They're *so* naughty that I can't seem to shake them, despite another virtuoso hip-swirl that makes me groan and claw his back.

"Back with us again, are we?" he gasps, laughing as he shags. He really is the most fabulous fuck.

"Yes! Yes!" It's half gasp, half cry, all genuine. I don't have to do a Meg Ryan when I'm with Terrence. He's just gorgeous and he knows how to do the business. And if that wasn't enough, he looks like a movie star, too. And not one of those mindless action hunks, mind you, all pecs and teeth and tan. No, he's like the more thoughtful kind of star, one with lots of gray cells, and a major-league sense of humor to go with his exceptional body.

And he's on top of me now, going like a jackhammer.

Or he was.

For a moment, he raises himself up on his elbows and looks down on me. His handsome face is sweaty and a little flushed, but that only makes him sexier than ever—and even hotter for the look in his eyes. They're narrowed, sort of cute but sly and shiver-inducingly knowing. He gives a little shake of his head as if he's read my mind. I hope he has, and I hope he likes what's in there.

He gives me a soft little kiss on the corner of my mouth. "Maybe I should go down on you again for a while. That'll stop you woolgathering while I'm giving you my fanciest moves, you naughty bitch." He licks his lips and that makes *him* look incredibly naughty.

You could spank me.

I open my mouth. I almost say it. But I don't. Not yet. That's a delicious treat I'm saving to surprise him with. Doesn't stop me thinking about it though.

"I like your moves. I love them!"

He tilts his head, and a comma of thick brown hair dangles in his eyes. "I should bloody well think so, woman." He smoothes my hair out of my eyes, too, and wipes the sweat from my brow. "You'd better brace yourself, because there's more of them incoming."

"Do your worst!" I growl, and he swirls again. "Or preferably, your best!"

I have to close my eyes now, because they're crossing from the pleasure of him this time, and either way, I must look like an idiot. Hitching around beneath him, I find an even better angle, if that's possible, and with another small kiss, then a bigger one, he starts to swing in and out again, with all the smooth power of a human reciprocating engine. Supporting himself on one arm, he strokes my body at the same time, his fingers as clever as his hips and cock are potent.

I start to rise higher, straining against him, arching, reaching, *savoring.*

And the naughty thoughts return to sweeten the climb.

In my mind, in a heartbeat, we're in a dark, dangerous room somewhere together. Is it a dungeon? Why, yes, it is... Here are the dingy, encrusted walls, the flickering torches in their sconces, the chains. And here's Terrence—though not quite the man who's currently fucking me. Well, he's the same, and just as sumptuous, but a darker version, more dangerous and exotic.

In bed, I grab at him, excitement building, my fluttering sex aroused anew by my kinky, yummy notions. "Baby," he growls, sensing every subtle and not-so-subtle response.

In my imaginary subterranean prison, he prowls around me, a slightly smiling figure all done up like the dream of a master. He's stripped to the waist, clad only in formfitting leather jeans and knee-high boots, apart from a platinum-studded collar round his neck. His hair is slicked back with water or gel or pomade, and his bare chest gleams in the torchlight as if he's oiled.

"Well, well, slave," he purrs in the mirror world.

Me, I'm strung up, my wrists in cuffs that dangle on chains from the smoky ceiling. *I'm* all done up like the dream of a slave, my body trussed in a corset of tight-laced satin, my feet in high-heeled pumps, a gag in my mouth.

A shudder runs through me in each parallel world, as he tweaks my nipple and makes me squirm.

Oh, god, he's so beautiful when he's stern. The mouth that kisses so softly is sculpted and cruel, and his warm brown eyes are black with power and lust.

As he slaps my bottom with the flat of his hand, I start to

come. And I come in the real world, too, in bed, lying underneath him. Straining for the best, the finest, the highest orgasm,
I arch against Terrence, my heels dragging against the backs of
his calves, my fingers flexing like talons, gripping his bottom.

I scream as I soar to heaven, while his phantom self smacks
my naked flesh, again and again.

Afterward, we lie against the pillows, both slumped and sweaty,
breathing hard. Multiple orgasms have knocked the stuffing
out of me, and even Terrence, with all his prodigious sexual
stamina, looks momentarily shattered.

"What the hell were you thinking, Vickie?" He turns to me,
and I see he's sharper and more with it than I imagined. Those
clever eyes of his gleam with knowledge, almost as if he really
were the master of my fantasy. "There was something dirty and
devious going on that turned you into a wildcat, wasn't there?"
He does that sinful lip-licking thing again. "Come on, woman,
tell the truth or you'll regret it." His mouth curves into a deliciously evil smile, and I'm back in heaven.

Oh, the threats... Oh, please bring them on!

Suddenly I'm not tired at all. Now's the time to tell him,
because I've a sneaky feeling he probably knows already. He's
got this uncanny knack of reading me, and it turns me on.

I prevaricate, gnawing my lip: an act, obviously.

"Vickie?" he prompts. There's a hint of sternness there, and
for a vertiginous second, I can't tell whether it's real or fabri-
cated. My pussy flickers again despite my previous surfeit of
pleasure.

"I...um...well, it was just a little fantasy I sometimes have."
Little? Who am I kidding? It's big and it's bad and it's beautiful.
"I...I don't mean that fucking you isn't satisfying...it's just I
have these thoughts sometimes." Lots of the time, and I'm dying

to share them. "I can't help myself, but it's not you, it's me. I...
You're a fabulous lover."

His eyes are on me. Steady and strangely bright. Knowing
again. The devil—he's teasing me. He's read my mind as easily
as if my eyes were made of glass. Suddenly he *is* the man in the
dungeon and twice as dangerous.

"But not quite fabulous enough," he growls, pursing his lips,
fighting that sunny, sexy "let's get it on" smile of his. "Spit it
out. What do you want? What dark and depraved perversion do
you think about when you're already having bloody good sex to
start with?"

I would point out to him that he has a very high opinion of
himself, but now's not the moment. Especially as I hold that
high opinion also.

"Well, you see...it's like this. I sort of like men to spank me.
It's a 'thing' of mine, you know?"

His eyes widen. He chews his lip. He looks perplexed. Oh,
give the man an Oscar! But he can't disguise the merriment in
his eyes.

"Good lord, you are a wicked little pervert, aren't you?"

"But I do like ordinary shagging too, honest! It's just that I
like spanking as well."

"I see." He's killing himself here. I swear he's dying to burst
out laughing.

"Perhaps I'd better go." Throwing myself into my penitent
role, I start to slide out of bed, ready to feign a search for my
scattered clothes.

But he stops me with a firm hand on my wrist. "Oh, no, you
don't! I think we need to get to the bottom of this." He has to
turn away then, and I can see his broad shoulders shaking. "I'm
going to get a bottle of wine. And then we'll discuss it properly.
No messing about."

Then he strides naked across the room, stalking toward the door, his gorgeous cock swinging. It's a bit perky again. More than perky.

Oh, god, I can't wait!

A few minutes later, after I've rushed to the bathroom and tidied my hair, I sneak back into the bedroom, and he's already returned.

But he's not in bed. Chin resting on his steepled fingers, he's sitting in the armchair, dressed again. Well, sort of. He's wearing his black jeans, but his chest and his feet are still bare. Whether by accident or design, he's managed to make himself even more magnificent than ever. He's the man of my dreams, literally and figuratively, and covering up his gorgeous goods only makes me feel more vulnerable by contrast.

"So, spanking, eh? There's a thing," he says, his voice level. He takes a measured sip of red wine from the glass that he's set on the bedside table at his elbow, and as he's staring at me, his smooth brow crinkles in a little manufactured frown.

I feel awkward, unsure of myself. This is all so real, all of sudden. Do I get back into bed? Or just sit on the edge of it? I feel off balance, standing here naked while he's sitting, clothed, and calmly drinking his wine.

He doesn't seem to have poured a glass for me.

"Yes...sorry. It's just a kink of mine. I can't help it."

His fine eyes narrow. Is he cross because I haven't shared this with him sooner? I start to feel shakier than ever, even though my pussy is already swimming.

"I never said there was anything wrong with it."

I'm starting to feel more and more disorientated, but in a good way. When I begin to edge toward the bed, he makes a little quirk of his lips that's so perfect it almost stops my heart. So I hover, feeling giddy, out of my depth.

He draws in a deep breath, sets aside his glass and stretches. "So, I suppose we could try a bit of this spanking. Give it a whirl."

My heart thuds madly. I feel a new rush of hot honey between my legs. If he really is what I suddenly suspect he is, I've hit the mother lode here.

He's Mister Perfectamundo. Everything I've ever wanted and a whole lot more.

"So, how does it go? What do you usually do?" He clasps his hands loosely in front of him, his head tipped slightly on one side, the glow from the lamp shining on his sleek dark hair.

"All sorts of things. Sometimes the man spanks me over his knee. Sometimes I lie across the bed, on my face, and he punishes me."

"What with? His hand? Or something else?"

We really are getting in deep here. Sliding through layers and layers. My heart flutters like a bat on crack. "Yes, sometimes his hand. Sometimes something like a belt, or even a leather slipper. Sometimes, um, toys."

"Toys?"

"Something like a spanking paddle...or a ruler...or even a riding crop."

Now, for some reason, I find it hard to look at him. His gaze is like a laser, sweeping over me.

"Fascinating." He pauses, a long slow beat. "But how do *you* want to start? What do you think is the best way to begin?"

My eyes are cast down. I stare at the carpet. But in my mind I can see his strong legs, his experienced thighs spread just the precisely right amount, his lap—with a growing bulge beneath the dark denim of his jeans. He's *become* his mirror self from my dungeon fantasy.

I drag in a breath with all the effort I would have to exert if the atmosphere had turned to water, or to gel. "I...I think I'd like you to spank me across your knee, if that's all right?"

"Yes, I think that would be okay." His voice is neutral, serene, soft. And yet humming with subliminal power. "But isn't there some kind of ceremony, a form of words at least? Don't you think it would be a good idea, maybe, to call me 'Master' or something?"

That thud in my heart picks up speed. I feel as if I'm in the middle of a vortex. "Y-yes, Master."

"Well, let's get started, shall we?"

Eyes still down, I pad across to him, and he offers a hand to help me go across him and assume the age-old position. His thighs feel firm and solid beneath the rough denim, his feet perfectly planted, everything in balance. As I go over, I feel safe. He won't let me fall.

As he adjusts his position slightly, and I adjust mine, his hand settles on the small of my back to steady me.

"You have a beautiful bottom, slave," he purrs quietly, with just a microsecond of artistic hesitation. That warm hand of his brushes my bare cheeks—first one, then the other. And then it moves again, stroking lightly, burning hot. I suppress a pathetic mewl when one finger traverses the length of my bottom crease.

"So, these men who spank you... Do they just play at it, or do they really spank you hard?"

"Yes. Sometimes quite hard." The words are difficult to get out. I can barely breathe.

"And do you like that?" He touches my anus and I squeak. Which he seems to ignore as a regrettable aberration.

"Yes! No! Sort of!" I can't see his face, but my imagination presents me with him smiling. Supreme. A happy god, playing with me in ways other than physical. But when he speaks, he still imbues his voice with that thread of theatrical doubt.

"Well, I'll have to see what I can do then. Wouldn't want to disappoint you after all this hard, serious spanking you've had in the past."

I open my mouth to protest that it isn't all that much, but then, out of the blue, his first smack lands and it just takes my words away.

It's not a heavy slap, but not light, either. It hurts. And it isn't by luck or blind intuition it's landed right on the crown of one bottom cheek. He knows exactly what he's doing, and has done all along.

"That's amazing," he says, sounding strangely awestruck.

That is *amazing,* I think, just struck.

He's hit me in the perfect place and with the perfect weight. Like Pavlov's dog, my body responds. My pussy ripples in anticipation of more, more, more and my lubrication starts to seep down onto his jeans. Unable to control myself, I wriggle and rub myself against him.

"Are you supposed to do that?" His voice is mildly questioning, but there's nothing unsure about the way his fingertips trace the hot hand-shaped mark they've just created. And there's nothing tentative about the way he slaps me again, on the other cheek this time.

I squeal, already out of control in a way I've never been before. But of course, I've never been with a master this experienced.

How on earth has it taken me this long to realize that fact?

"I'll bet you're not supposed to do that, either," he remarks, sounding joyful, as if he's really enjoying getting into the swing of things. His arm certainly is, because he's slapping steadily now. If I had brain cells left over to ponder such matters, I'd wonder what on earth I'd done to deserve this bounty, a man

with a perfect natural gift for corporal punishment and a beau-
tifully honed skill. But I have very little brainpower available
at the moment, nothing left over from the writhing, the whimpering and the blatant and desperate way I massage my crotch
against his hard thigh.

He smacks and smacks. I squirrel around and sob. And what
happens eventually is almost inevitable, I suppose.

It all gets too much for me, and hitching myself up a bit, I
sneak a hand beneath myself and slither fingers into my pussy.
While he's still spanking me, I find my clit and rub it fever-
ishly.

After that, I'm a lost cause, and within seconds, I climax
hard. Very hard. Almost too hard. I jackknife on his knee,
almost fall off, but he holds me tight. My pleasure soars as his
fingers press my tender redness.

I fall back into my body again as a sniveling, glowing, still-
pulsing, incredibly happy mess. As I half slide and half fall in
a guided fashion to the carpet at his feet, he reaches into his
pocket and then hands me a handkerchief.

"You've done that a hundred times before, you sly brute,
haven't you?" I accuse him from my lowly position as my brain
clicks back into operating mode and I start to grin. "All that
BS about making me tell you what my fantasies are... You've
known all along. You could read the signs, couldn't you?
Why didn't you tell me you were into exactly the same thing
as me?"

He cups my face, makes me look up at him. His eyes are
radiant with knowledge and mischief and power, utterly
entrancing, although there's a base part of me that's more interested in his enormous erection and is dying to check that out.

"I suppose I should say sorry for stringing you along," he
says softly, the stroke of his finger beneath my chin an elegant

counterpoint to the throbbing in my bottom and in my pussy, "but a master doesn't usually apologize, does he?"

The M-word makes the pulsation between my legs deeper, hotter—even though it's barely minutes since I came. "No, but you still could have told me," I persist, wondering and hoping that if I provoke him enough he might do more.

"Indeed...indeed I could." His beautiful eyes glitter with excitement, danger, desire and dominance, holding me utterly as he goes on to remind me of the party where we met, and how he sought me out. I'd wondered why he, this peach of a man, had selected me when there were much sexier girls on the prowl. I'm pretty enough, but I know I'm a quiet bloomer.

"You're right. I *could*—I can—read you. I could tell you shared my interests...it's patently obvious from the way you carry yourself." I shudder at the thought of me beaming out those secret signals, an open book to a *cognoscento* like Terrence. "So I decided to see how long it would take for you to admit it."

"Oh, for heaven's sake! You devious bastard!"

"Tut tut...naughty, naughty," he chides, but the look in his eyes makes me wetter and warmer than ever, "Why so cross? It's what you wanted, isn't it? Part of the game? The dance?"

I want to maintain my mega-defiance act, play at being aggrieved, but the greater part of me, the truer part of me is thrilled, light-headed. He *is* my ideal, and I can't believe my luck.

"Um...yes, I suppose," I answer with a last mulish flicker.

"Finally, she admits it. I should punish you for being so obstinate, shouldn't I?"

My heart lurches. Can my steaming bottom take it? So soon? When I'm so red, so sore? But my sex lurches, too, gathering itself and readying. I almost come, without a touch, at the thought of more.

"Yes, Master," I whisper, lowering my head in acknowledgment, and starting to shuffle into position in order to get up and across his knee again.

"Oh no, Vickie...not that. Well, not right at the moment." He adjusts his own position now, conveying an eloquent message, and gilding it with a gentle but still delightfully devilish smile.

Oh, yummy, I think, reaching out to lower his zipper.

GUESS

Charlotte Stein

I know he's there, because I can smell him. It's that cherry lip gloss he knows I like, though god knows where he's put it. On his lips? Too conventional. On his nipples? They're small and perky and would look delicious coated in something slippery, but I doubt it.

I'm betting on his cock; undoubtedly on his cock. And while I'm lying here blindfolded and largely helpless, he's going to make me taste it—that cherry-scented, cherry-flavored curve of flesh.

I can just picture him now, getting closer, with it bobbing between his thighs. His breath is unsteady, though his resolve seems to be holding, and every now and then I can hear him, moving in close.

There's just that hint of *too* close, like maybe he can't quite help himself.

I think that sets me off more than the blindfold—that sense of his bucking arousal, trying to lunge at me. How it excites

him to the point of teeth baring and flushed cheeks, to think of
me cut off like this: entirely unable to tell what he's going to do
next; not sure which body part he's touching me with.

Is that his finger, trailing over the curve of my hip? I'm spread
out on the bed, legs wide to show off my already glistening pussy,
so there's plenty for him to go after. But he chooses just that tiny
innocuous spot, with the edge of something light and small.

And then I feel something moist and sudden, against the
squeamish inside of my right elbow.

Of course, the rational part of me tells me it's his tongue,
but my mind has long since stopped playing in that ball pool. I
think of things jellied and weird—wild sex toys that self-lubri-
cate, alien fingers getting ready to probe.

Before long it goes away again, and all I can do is cry for
more. I don't care if it *is* an alien finger. I *want* to be probed. My
skin feels so hot and tight, I'm sure he could just peel it right off
my body if he wanted to, and between my legs is a taut, waiting
sensation.

My pussy wants to know, desperately, why he's making me
cling to nothing and come apart for so little.

But I know why. I always know why. It's because he wants
me to guess.

I try *moist towelette,* but he just laughs. He laughs as high and
tight as I feel, and tells me, "Wrong, Vy, so wrong. Try again."

And then something as soft as breath stirs over my right
nipple, so almost-not-there, it's excruciating. My entire body
gravitates toward it, but as I'm canting one way he somehow
gets over me and tickles the other nipple.

Feather, I think, and say so.

"Come on, come on," I say. "It's a feather, a feather, I win!"

But either the guess isn't right or he's a liar. I think he's a
liar. He's doing this on purpose, so I'll never win. I'll have to

stay blindfolded forever, wet and wanting, clit standing stiff and proud and just waiting for him to have some mercy.

However, I know he won't. It'll be something coy, against that tender place. Something slim and barely there, and made out of ice so that I tear and pull at the bedsheets, when he finally presses it to my bud.

But he's a changeable, tricky sort, because instead, he trails something stuttering and sticky over my right cheek. Really he shouldn't have, because it's far too easy to guess. I can feel him shifting, very close to my head. I can smell the musky scent of him, made strong with precome and the sweat that will definitely be glossing his belly now.

It'll be pooling at the hollow of his back; behind his knees, too, I know, because I saw it all when I did this exact same thing to him. He had trembled, though, and I don't think I'm trembling, yet. He had called out hoarsely, and begged me before I even got to crueler things, but I stay silent, apart from the guessing.

In fact, I think he's trembling more than I am, and making more noise, even with the roles reversed. His cock slithers over my cheek, too jerkily. The pillow feels like it's juddering under my head, and I wonder if that's due to the knee he's got pressed into it.

I think about him strung as taut as I currently am, and a flood of wetness makes itself known between my legs. My clit jumps, my belly fills up with tingles, and when he skirts a little bit too close, I stick out my tongue and catch the tip of his cock, just as I knew I would.

I can never resist, or play the game properly. Not when he tastes so salty and slick. Not when he groans so prettily for me, low and throaty.

Guess, I think. *Guess what I'm going to do next.*

I think he goes with *She's going to try to suck my cock*, because he moves away after a moment of reluctance, calling me a bad girl as he does. He makes an effort to force his words into a true reproach, too, but they waver too much for that. There's an up and down note in them that sounds a little like laughter, and a lot like arousal.

I love him for those twin things. They go together so well, though I never thought they would. He has a bright, sharp grin like a curving knife, and when he flashes it at me I'd do anything. I'd spread my pussy for him, my ass, just anything, anything he wanted.

I can tell what he wants, right now. He says, hoarsely, "Guess what this is."

And I resist the urge to complain. I can hear his hand all slick on his cock, back and forth, back and forth, and I know what's going to happen. He's going to come all over me, before we're even halfway through playing.

No self-restraint. I'd call him a disappointment, but then again he knows how much I love hearing him go at himself. He's moaning before he's gotten to the third stroke, and then he pants out dirty words for me to delight in.

"Oh, god, you look so hot all tied up like that. Really hot. Spread your legs so I can look at your pussy."

It's not really part of the game, and my legs are kind of spread anyway, but I do it just the same. I spread them as wide as they'll go, and then picture him staring hungrily at my glistening folds—because, by god, are they ever glistening. I can feel my wetness sliding into the crack of my ass, and everything down there feels sticky and swollen.

Even if I couldn't tell that myself, I'd know it from his reaction. He grunts, gutturally, and that slick shuttling sound speeds up—oh, does he really think I can't guess what he's doing? I hope he understands that I can always guess, when it comes to this particular thing. He doesn't even need to touch me.

I always know when he's masturbating. It's kind of how we came together in the first place, because we were friends and then one day we went camping, and by chance we had to share a tent. He thought he was being sly, in the darkness, in the middle of the night.

But I guessed right off what he was doing. I knew even while dreaming, as my unconscious mind led me down naughty paths filled with hot guys moaning, breathlessly; hot guys licking their palms then circling their big, hard cocks...oh. He knows what I like, all right.

Could be that this half of the game isn't even about guessing, really. It's about knowing. Knowing what will drive me wild and make me strain against the silly scarves he's got around my wrists. I tell him to do it louder, louder, but of course he doesn't obey. He gets his voice low and tight, and I have to fight to hear him.

"Yeah," he whispers. "Yeah, look how wet and swollen you are. Oh, yeah, I just want to fuck that tight little cunt."

He's a bastard—though no more of a bastard than I am. I made him guess with my pussy all over his face. I made him guess until he cried—though only because I know that's what he likes.

We're too wrapped up in each other to ever play this game properly, now. Why guess, when you know?

And he does know. He tells me he's going to come all over my clit, which is definitely not part of the rules. He's not supposed to *tell* me what he's going to do, but he does so anyway, because he gets how much it turns me on. My hips buck without my permission, and I make a strangled sound when usually I can stay silent no matter what.

His come all over my pussy? All over my clit? Just thinking about it makes me want to snap these stupid scarves and attack him. If I bend my thumb a certain way and close my fist, I think I can get out of at least one of them. I can, I know I can.

But of course, I don't. At the last second, I hold myself back. I wait for him to push himself over that final hurdle, to get so excited and so worked up that he just has to spurt between my spread legs.

And he does. He even apologizes while he's doing it. He tells me that he's sorry, he can't stop himself, he just has to come. Then he announces his coming, in desperate, grating tones— oh, those words. Those two words. *I'm coming. I'm coming.*

I don't know which is better: hearing him give in and use my body like that, or feeling the hot splash of it right over my clit, just as he promised. He's good like that. At keeping his promises, I mean.

And then when he's done, and the room is full of the sounds of his pleasure dissipating—rough and ragged breath, guilty sighs—I feel that slickness sliding down between my legs. The edges of my orgasm flutter close, from nothing more than that slippery sensation.

Though him talking brings it closer, I have to say.

"Oh, you look all messy now," he says. There's a hint of tease behind the regret in his voice. I think I like that, best of all. Or maybe I like it more when he tells me, "Guess. Guess what I've done to you, dirty girl."

I love him, I love him, I love him.

"I don't have to guess," I say, but he makes me. He makes me by keeping me on that fluttering edge of my orgasm.

"All right," I choke out, finally. I sound bitter, but I don't feel it. "You've just done it on me."

"What have I done?"

He usually sounds so bright and open. Most of the time he's like a big kid, boyish and enthusiastic about every little thing. But now he sounds darkly pleased, like he's got me right where he wants me. I should really tell him—you can have me there, anytime.

"You've..." I struggle to think of the right term. All of them sound childish. "You've spunked on me."

That sounds the most childish, of all of them. I should have gone with *come,* but it's too late now. He laughs, and I fight against the scarves. *You fucker,* I want to tell him, but I don't mean it.

"Yeah," he says. "Yeah, I guess I have. I guess you win, Pol."

Oh. I hadn't thought of that. I was too busy thinking *you fucker,* to process that he was actually going to hand over the reins. I win, and so now I get to do what I want and say what I want and make him, make him, make him.

Which is what I like best of all, I know I do. So how come I don't demand that he untie me? How come I don't tell him to remove the blindfold? I can't say. I'm not sure. Instead I just whine and wait for him to understand exactly what I want.

And of course, he does. He's my Stu. He always understands.

He leans down before I've uttered a word and kisses the place he's made a mess of. His mouth feels searing hot where the thick, unbearable liquid is cooling, and I don't know what turns me on more, the fact that he's licking my clit, or the idea that he doesn't give a crap about tasting his own come.

I've had boyfriends who refused to do this or that or the other—but that's just not him. He never refuses to do anything; in truth, I don't even have to ask. He just licks and licks and giggles at the taste, until I sink my teeth into my lower lip and grip the scarves as tightly as I can.

My clit feels huge under his tongue, and it's not a surprise that it hardly takes anything to make me come. I feel like I've been standing at that edge for an age, and all he has to do is circle my clit once or twice, maybe slip a finger into me, maybe make a sound that vibrates right through me and oh. Oh. Bliss spreads through my lower body, so sweet and fine.

It gets a good grip on me and I struggle against it, briefly, but the feel of his big hands around my thighs, suddenly, and his tongue pressed firm and flat to my clit—yeah, that keeps me in it. I give everything I have over to it.

To him.

God, what it is to have a man who always knows, and never guesses.

HER, HIM,
AND THEM

Aimee Pearl

er

On our first date, she says, "I already told you, I'm not into that S-and-M stuff." She says it hard, with an edge of determined anger rather than annoyance or exasperation. My panties get wet from the tone in her voice, and that's how I know she is lying.

We leave the restaurant and go back to her place. Soon, we are all over each other, fingers and hands dancing with buttons and hems. When her fingers are inside me, she instructs, "Don't come yet." Later she says, "Okay, now," and I come for her on command, without hesitation.

Later still, with her inside me, she says, "If you're gonna come, ask me first."

I still don't get it, the underlying meaning of her words. Softly, lustily, I murmur, "Yes, okay."

A short time after that, I come, hard, while she is fucking me from behind. She leans in close and soft, her front pressing against my back, her hand caressing my hair.

"Baby," she whispers, gentle and sweet, "did you come?"

"Yes," I sigh.

Slam!

She grabs my hair hard by the fistful and shoves my face viciously into the pillow. "Didn't I tell you to ask first?" comes her fervent growl. I suddenly get it and snap into submissive mode.

"I'm sorry."

"I didn't ask you if you were sorry. Do you remember that I told you to ask first?"

"Yes."

"So why didn't you do as you were told?"

Her angry energy is enough to make me come again, as I beg and plead. "I forgot, it just felt so good, I couldn't help it, please, I'm sorry..."

Much later that night, she says, "I like telling girls what to do. And girls seem to like to be told. Why is that? Why do girls like that?"

"Because it's so relaxing..."

On our second date, we go to a local lesbian club. I had emailed her earlier that day, telling her I had a fantasy that I wanted to fulfill. It involved the club's bathroom and her packing a dildo. When I get to the club, I can't tell at first if she is packing for me, but after a few minutes, she takes my hand and discreetly leads it to her crotch. Electricity shoots through both of us as I caress the stiff cock that lies against her thigh.

We watch the club's go-go dancer, feeding dollar bills into her G-string and sipping our drinks just long enough to tease each other. About an hour into the evening, I take her hand and say, "Come with me." Silently, we walk back to the bathroom, music thumping all around us, bodies pressed close as we squeeze through the crowd.

As we wait in line, she hands me a condom; we kiss, touch and tease. Someone comes out of the bathroom, and in we go. We enter it boldly, in front of the whole dance floor, like it is nothing at all.

She locks the door behind us and gives one command.

"Turn around."

I obey and put one hand on the sink ledge and one on the toilet tank. The bathroom is filthy in a sexy way, with debris on the ground.

She pulls down my pants in a swift motion. I stay motionless for her. Neither of us utters a word. I sigh and wet myself as I hear her unbuckle and unzip.

There is a pause, then she roughly pulls my G-string to one side of my lips and shoves inside me.

I groan.

Someone rattles the door, trying to get in. We ignore it. She fucks me quick and dirty.

"Lift up. I want to see your face."

I raise up enough for her to see my expression in the mirror on the wall nearest the toilet.

"Play with yourself."

She is going hard and deep. I thrash around, still a touch sore from last night, on every downstroke. I make noise, and she doesn't tell me to be quiet. Heaven.

Abruptly, and without warning, she pulls out. She pulls her pants down some and sits on the nasty toilet, without wiping it first. This turns me on even more, but I'm not sure what she wants from me. I start to pull up my pants.

"Why are you doing that?" she asks in a voice that is more instruction than question.

I pull them back down and, in one quick move, as she starts to pee, she tugs the string to the side again and shoves three fingers inside. Three is my magic number. She fucks me hard while she pees, and she pees for a long time.

My face is even closer to the mirror now, and I watch myself come, crying out loudly, as she curls those fingers inside me and coaxes at my spot.

I finish coming as the last of her drops hit the bowl.

She wipes, I don't.

We both pull our pants up. "Ready?" she asks. I nod, and we walk back outside.

Soon after that, we leave the club and walk back to her house, holding hands. At her place, we get into bed. I am still dressed; she is down to her boxers.

"Aren't you going to take off your clothes?" she asks.

"No, I want you to take them off of me."

"No."

We both pause. I lean over her like a cat.

"Take them off," she orders.

Reluctantly, I comply, removing my pants and shirt. Now I am just in my G-string. I lie down beside her.

"Why are you still wearing this?" She plucks at the fabric, fingering the string along my hip. I don't answer.

"What's it for?" she asks. "Why do you need to wear it to sleep? I mean, it's just a piece of string."

I don't answer.

"What's it for?" she asks again, in a more exasperated tone.

On her breath intake, I half-interrupt, slowly asking, "Do you like it?"

Right on the tail of my question, but in a calmer voice, she replies, "Yes, I like it. I like it a lot."

I whisper close, slow and low: "That's what it's for."

In the darkness, she smiles and wraps her presence more tightly around me.

"You're smart," she says, forehead against mine. I curl into her arm and rub my leg along her thigh. She knows what I want.

"I'm going to sleep," she says. "I'm not going to have sex with you."

I protest with my body.

"No."

"You're mean," I complain. I hear her chuckle, but her resolve continues. I pause, then whisper, "Please, I just want to show you one thing. Please."

Very slowly and reluctantly, she gives me her hand and lets me lead it under the band of my panties, until her fingers are pressed flat against my lips. I am soaking wet, and she moans louder than I do upon this discovery. She caresses my lips, and we are both breathless. Her finger slips easily between the folds of my flesh, and I remember that she had told me the night before that she likes to fist women. I want her whole hand inside, and my body tenses and coils—greedy—around that one finger.

"How do you do that?" she asks of my wetness.

"You did it," I reply.

She slides her finger out of me, then slides her hand out from under the fabric. I cling to her, moaning, and again she says, "No."

"I'm going to sleep," she says. "I'm not going to fuck you."

My leg wraps around her thigh and her hand finds its way to my clavicle.

She whisper-growls, "I'm not going to fuck you. I'm not going to fuck you."

"You're already fucking me," I tell her. "When you put your hand around my throat, you're fucking me. When you let me ride your thigh like this, you're fucking me."

Her hand moves higher and tighter, higher and tighter, until I stop moving on her leg entirely, lost in the sounds of my breathing, sharp intakes.

Her hand gets tighter still, and even as I struggle against it, prying at it with my fingers, I have no fear.

When my breathing slows, she gradually moves her hand away and turns from me. I leave in the morning before she wakes up, feeling bittersweet and still hoping to find someone to take me there.

Him

On our first date, he takes me for a walk on the pier. It is late at night, but there are fishermen everywhere, with their teenage sons, radios and bait. We walk to the far end of the pier and begin to kiss.

He is everywhere at once, grabbing at my tits and pinching my nipples through the sheer, silky fabric of my blouse. Our backs are to the fishermen, as he rubs and ruts his hips against my ass.

He comes around front. "Show me your tits," he demands.

"I'm shy," I lie.

He takes my tits out of my shirt for me; looks and likes what he sees.

A while later, we decide to go back to his place. Before we turn to go, he takes them out again, sliding the folds of material underneath my breasts. "Walk like this with me."

"No way! They'll see," I reply, incredulous, nodding toward the fishermen and their sons in the distance.

"Just two steps. Good girl. Such a good girl."

I am throbbing wet and do as I am told. After a couple of steps, we are nearing the lamppost, and my breasts are visible to any man who might turn around from his fishing line toward us. He lets me cover up with my jacket.

I am sizzling hot; the cool night breeze kisses my cheeks and makes me smile. Finally, I'm getting there.

Them

Elias is a present from Him. He and I haven't seen each other in a couple of weeks, so He's ready and aching to fuck me. He brings his friend Elias to help. He'll hold me down by the arms while Elias has his way with me.

I'm nervous that His friend won't be my type, won't be attractive to me. On the phone before they come over, I tell Him, "I'll do whatever you tell me to do; I'll use my safeword if I have to, but otherwise, you're in charge." I know it'll be more fun for me that way.

He and Elias come over, and all my anxieties are relieved: Elias is gorgeous. They come in my kitchen, and He orders me to make tea for them. As I move around the room, He catches me and lifts my skirt. I have to show my ass and then, later, my pussy. He pulls my tits out of my shirt, for Elias to see. He bends me over his knee and spanks me, to show off.

As they have their tea, I'm instructed to kneel and remove their boots. I do so. He and Elias get up as I lean over the sink, washing up; they come behind me, grabbing me and forcing my hands behind my back. He traces my hands over the outline of Elias's huge, hard cock, straining through his jeans. I can't believe the size!

He and Elias are done with tea and ready to fuck me. We go into my bedroom. I strip on command and spend hours and hours servicing them, getting fucked by them, being held down, beaten, slapped, spit on, and violated by them. The condoms pile up on the floor by the bed; the lube bottle is almost empty by morning.

Elias has coarse fingertips at the ends of his strong hands, and he has day-old stubble that rubs my cheek, shoulders and back, everywhere he chooses to kiss, lick and bite. Every touch feels good, even when he grabs my ankles and roughly spreads my legs apart. Every time Elias's cock enters me, with his fingers in my ass, I come hard. I'm satiated by these two men: soft skin taut over hard muscle, the push and pull of my lovers.

We three fuck for hours and hours and hours. Elias blazes beside me. I am heat and water at the same time. A goddess lying between two minions, I submit with more depth and grace than I would have imagined. They lift me.

In the early morning hours, Elias chokes me gently, with a soft, knowing strength. I have *never* let a man put his hand to my neck before in that way. Later in the morning, as He snores to my right, Elias and I caress on the left. Elias whispers to me, as his fingers trace lazy circles over my clit, "Your body makes me nervous."

"My body makes you nervous? Why?"

"Because it's so beautiful. You have the kind of body that, if someone wanted to trap me, this would be the bait. It's gorgeous. I would be trapped."

"What do you like about it?"

"This soft amber-colored skin, these tits with dark-brown nipples, your incredible ass, the way your pussy is neatly tucked into itself...I would be trapped."

Later still that morning, with Him watching us, I trap Elias again, in the sticky web of my cunt, and we come together.

BAYOU

Clancy Nacht

The heavy scent of river and sweet smell of flowers wafts into the open window, circling my silk robe around my body. I love this moment in the night; love the breeze from the fans, buffeting my skin with its soft caress.

I hear my lover behind me. The ice clinks in his glass. Scotch: I can smell it from here, but it never smells as good on the air as it does on his lips, from his breath. I let my white robe drift down from my shoulders, like a slow-floating cloud. It slips from my arms and down to show him the cleavage of my ass, the dark shadow meant to allure him.

His clothes shift, the chair creaks. His footfalls draw him nearer. I feel the heat of his body, the smell of his cologne. The stubble is hard on my shoulder as he looks out onto the Mississippi, his cheek against mine.

My building is so dilapidated, it's crumbling from the inside. Bricks wake me in the night, loosening and falling down to the dusty floor.

But he is not crumbling, nor will he. He presses his highball glass to the lower part of my spine, and I whimper. My skin prickles with sensation, the fine hairs pointing upward to catch the wind as it blows over my body. From the front, I am an eyeful for anyone who might peer up through my window. My breasts are large and swing slowly with each movement. My hips are wide, giving ample definition to the line of my pubis.

At his grunt, I drop the fabric and it slides to the floor in a pool at my feet.

He pulls a piece of ice from his drink and slides it down my spine, starting at the nape. My hair is wound up in a loose bun on my head, giving him access.

It is so cold I can barely stand it, but then, it is so soothing on this sweltering night. The ice draws a line down my spine, tracing lightly at every groove on its way down.

His hand presses on the center of my back, urging me forward. I grip the windowsill. My reflection gazes back at me as I spread my legs for him, letting him see all he wants of me.

I don't dare look back at him. It ruins the moment.

I must always look forward, stare into space.

He draws the line of the ice along my lower back, filling in the space with swirls, light touches. He repeats it long enough to hear me moan, to watch my spine rise trying to get more of the cold tip of the ice. My skin flinches, shrinking from his fingers as he strokes the ice along my body.

Just a sliver in his hand, he dips it between my asscheeks; I jump. I've never felt the chill of ice on my anus; never felt it swirling around my opening like that.

The confused sensations make me shiver; such a warm area suddenly flushing with cold. And he moves it down, down, down to that sensitive skin between.

My pussy clenches in anticipation.

I want to feel it there. I dread the absolute cold of the ice, but I want the pure sensation. I want to feel the chill of it on my hot opening. I want to take it inside of me and turn it into nothing but water.

He stands above me, leaning over me so that his warm chest is pressed to my back, which is slick from the heat and sensations prickling through my body. He reaches between my legs from behind, fucking me with the sliver of ice—swirling it around the opening, teasing the clenching muscles, making it shrink back. He pulls it away until my pussy throbs for it.

Each time the ice gets near me, my sex clenches, trying to capture it.

His other hand kneads my breast, massaging it as he whispers how beautiful I am. Picking up a new cube from the drink, he pushes it halfway inside my cunt.

Once it's through the hole, I can barely feel it unless it touches the hot, pulsing walls inside of me. I squeeze around it, tilting my hips back trying to get more. I want the ice deeper inside of me. I want more.

He pulls away to walk to the old fridge. It whirs at the edge of my loft. He keeps things in there, things I don't look at because I like the surprise. It is a long, glass dildo that he fishes from his long, black box.

Condensation forms the moment he pulls it from the freezer.

I watch how he moves toward me in his suit. The top few buttons are undone, his tie hangs loosely around his neck. His dark hair is neatly combed, a bare stubble on his face.

He moves behind me, holding the tip of the chilled dildo at my opening. He teases my clit with it; circles my anus; but finally settles on my open, wet pussy, pressing it slowly inside.

At first, it feels like everything has gone numb in reaction to the ice-cold spike being driven through me. But my body warms it or becomes accustomed to it. Either way, all of my nerves are alive, on edge.

He kisses my back, fucking me slowly with the glass dildo as I moan and push back against it for more, the edges of my opening relishing the new cold as it goes deeper.

I hear his zipper, the rustle of fabric. I hear the liquid sound of the tube of lubricant spitting and the slick of a condom sliding on. The blunt weight of his cock pressures my ass.

I inhale.

As I exhale, he thrusts smoothly inside of me.

We rest there as we both adjust to the sensation.

His lips softly caress my ear with a swirl of breath. "I can feel the cold inside of you. I can feel it inside the walls of your body."

I rest my forehead on the windowsill, luxuriating in being so full, in the contrast of the cold dildo and the thick heat of his cock. They move inside of me, each radiating its own energy, trying to touch each other through the wall of my body. I shift on my feet, angling myself to get him where I want him, to that spot where his cock and the dildo move together, scratching an itch so deep inside that it's never been touched.

I'm stretched wide open for him and his toy—exposed and hungry for it, using it to feed the mounting lust that burns for being filled like this.

The night air is muggy like death. A dog barks outside. A car drives by and no one knows what is going on in my room. No one suspects that I am right there, through the thin pane of a window with my lover's cock in my ass, a cold dildo inside of my cunt.

I'm so excited, I can hardly breathe.

I rub my clit. He presses an ice cube against my arm and

I take it, using it to rub myself off. The cold is more than my clit can handle. I picture the soft pink flesh rubbing against the slick clear rectangle and I start to tremble above and beyond the cold.

I'm so close and I just want to hear his voice. "Tell me you want me."

"God, yes. I want you. I want you to make me come like this."

The pleasure rolls over me like the lapping of waves, coming in slowly, cresting, connecting me to the world as my body fights for that ultimate release. I can hear my breathing and nothing else.

I exhale and the air grows denser from the steaminess of my breath.

I let go, feeling the pulses wrapped around the toy, sending the shock waves through my anus so that it clenches around him until he comes, too. He places his drink on the floor to knead my breasts as we twitch, milking the last of our releases, trying to ride it out for as long as we can.

He pulls me up, fingers pinching my nipples. Then he grabs my arm to twirl me around. Then he kisses me. It's the first time I've looked into his eyes all night. And the last for tonight.

I tell him that I love him.

He smiles and finishes his scotch.

Then he leaves.

SMOKE

Elizabeth Coldwell

I really, really need a smoke.

I'm in the middle of yet another attempt at cutting down—not giving up. I've tried that and failed so many times, I know it's never going to happen. Instead, I try to go as long as I can without giving in to my cravings. And I'd been doing so well, until now.

Two things are always guaranteed to make me want a cigarette. One is sex. My first instinct, once the last sweet waves of orgasm die away, is to roll over and light up. Not that I'm inconsiderate in these matters. I've lost count of the number of times I've wrapped a sheet around myself and padded out onto the balcony of the flat to smoke in satisfied postcoital solitude.

The other is beer. That's why I knew I was in trouble as soon as I walked into the bar. But after a long, tedious couple of hours spent tramping round the Rijksmuseum, while the guide droned on about every last nuance of every last Rembrandt masterpiece, I was more than ready for a glass of something cold and bitter.

A couple of minutes' walk away are the tourist traps of the Leidseplein, packed and noisy in the hot June sun. Holland has been playing in a World Cup match this afternoon, so it seems half the people crowded around the pavement tables are decked out in the team's traditional orange. It makes an arresting spectacle, but a friend at work told me I should bypass the bars on the square in favor of this place, hidden down an unremarkable side street.

It seemed a little dingy as I walked in, but maybe that was just my eyes adjusting after the brightness outside. Gradually, I've come to appreciate its not inconsiderable charms: wood-paneled walls and furniture, stained even darker than their original brown by exposure to years of nicotine; tea lights flickering in heavy red glass jars on every table; posters celebrating the output of a dozen breweries across the Low Countries. And, most importantly, a beer menu every bit as extensive as my friend promised.

After careful consideration, I plumped for a bottle of geuze, dry and deliciously sour in taste. The barman, who couldn't be any older than twenty-one, went through the ritual of washing an already perfectly clean glass before pouring the beer with a flourish. As I relished the first sip, he adjusted the sound system, swapping it from a loop of bland Euro-ballads to low, dirty rock music, the kind whose bass line makes a direct connection to your crotch, impossible to ignore.

So now I'm not just ready for a cigarette, I'm getting horny, too. It doesn't help that the barman is rather cute, very tall and very blond, with traces of puppy fat still clinging to his cheeks. Maybe he's a little young for me, but that doesn't stop me looking and silently lusting.

Mind you, Amsterdam has far more than its share of hot blonds. Like the policeman keeping a watchful eye on the

Leidseplein crowds, his uniform trousers clinging to his ass in a way that makes me yearn for him to press me up against a wall and frisk me. I'm sure that's not a tactic favored by the Dutch police, but still my mind revisits the scene, fantasizing about the moment when he kicks my legs a little farther apart so he can pat his way up my jeans-clad thighs, closer and closer to my pussy...

I shake my head to clear it of the thought and take another swig of my beer. It doesn't help, because now sex is firmly on my mind. Just round the corner from here is a day spa and sauna. Passing it earlier, I saw another good-looking blond going inside. He didn't notice me, and even if he had, I doubt I would have registered with him. The tight white underwear and accessories for sale in the window made it very clear this spa is for gay men—the memory of which only plants a whole new set of images in my mind. Men, lolling on the benches in the heat of the sauna, pulling aside towels to display their rapidly stiffening cocks. Long, muscled thighs being spread widely, so a blond head can bob obediently between them, mouth sucking hard...

I shift on my stool, aware that the seam of my jeans is pressing insistently against my pussy lips. The barman catches my eye and smiles, as though he's reading my thoughts and knows just how turned on I am. It's no good. I fumble through my bag, searching for the packet of cigarettes and lighter I've stashed firmly at the bottom, so as not to tempt me.

In common with most cities these days, Amsterdam has very strict rules on lighting up in public, and so I make my way to the little terrace outside. There's one table, big enough for half a dozen people to sit around it. When I arrived, there was a group here, all dressed in orange and celebrating Holland's victory, but now only two lads in their late twenties remain.

One of them is drinking Kwak; I recognize the distinctive,

round-bottomed glass at once, held suspended in a stout wooden frame. A colleague once ordered a bottle on a night out back home and had to leave his shoe behind the bar to guarantee he'd return the glass. There's no such system in place here. Maybe the Dutch are more trustworthy, or maybe it's just no longer a novelty.

Neither he nor his friend appear to pay much attention as I emerge from the bar's dark interior. They're chatting away in rapid Dutch, interspersed with the odd raucous laugh. I study them covertly as I flip a cigarette from the pack. Kwak Boy has tousled dark hair and a growth of stubble on his broad jaw. His companion is fairer, with a cynical cast to his foxy features. I wouldn't turn either of them down, but I'm not vain enough to automatically assume they'd be interested in a woman my age.

The flint on the lighter strikes, but fails to ignite. I try a couple more times, growing increasingly frustrated.

"Do you need a light?" the fair-haired lad asks in impeccable English.

"That'd be great, thanks."

He produces a lighter, quickly kindling a flame from it. I lean close, inhaling as the cigarette lights and tasting the first welcome lungful of smoke.

That's one of my imminent needs sorted, but not the other. The pulse still beating steadily deep between my legs is proof of that.

"You're on holiday here?" the other man asks. I can't help but notice he's not looking me in the eyes as he speaks. His gaze is lower, fixed on the point where my olive-green T-shirt stretches across my breasts. Even in my forties, I'm lucky enough to be able to get away without a bra on sultry days like this, and he's making the most of the sight of my nipples poking hard against the soft-brushed cotton.

"Yes." I accept the unspoken invitation to sit, to make conversation, perching on the edge of the bench.

"Your first time?"

I shake my head. "I've been here a couple of times before, but I've never found this bar till now."

"You've missed a treat. Gijs and I almost never drink anywhere else. I'm Peter, by the way."

"Barbara."

He takes my hand, holding it for a fraction longer than is socially polite. I'm wondering if there's more than just friendliness behind his eagerness to make small talk, whether I'm reading the flirtatious looks he's giving me correctly. His next words remove any doubt from my mind.

"You have fantastic tits, Barbara. I said that to Gijs when we first saw you."

Gijs takes a long swallow of his blond beer before adding, "That's not all he said. He reckoned you were pretty fuckable, too."

There are two ways the conversation can go from here. I can quickly finish my smoke and scuttle back inside, flattered but ignoring the obvious proposition. Or I can—as I do—make eye contact with Gijs and suck on the cigarette as though it's a miniature cock.

There's something I need to know before this goes any further. "When I arrived here, you were sitting with three girls." I picture them in my mind, young and pert, attractive in a wholesome, farmer-folk way, like the barman inside. "If you're in the mood for a fuck, what was wrong with them?"

Gijs shrugs. "They don't do it for me. I like someone older, someone who knows what she wants." He leans closer. "Tell me, Barbara, what do *you* want?"

I want what I've wanted since my first sip of beer, since the music started to rouse me on some primitive level: to be filled with hot, hard cock. More than that, I want to try something I would only dare in a foreign country, where I know there's absolutely no chance of bumping into someone I know who wouldn't approve, or understand.

"You and Peter. At the same time. And we've got to be quick, because I've left my beer sitting on the bar. How about it?" As my words hang in the air, I can't believe I've been so bold. Playing for such high stakes has never really appealed to me before.

Peter spins his empty bottle on the table. Is he deciding whether to go for it or not? A quick glance between the two men, then they nod.

Gijs extends a hand to me. "Come on."

Halfway down the street, there's a little alleyway between a low, modern block of flats and the older, more traditionally gabled building next to it. Gijs pulls me into the darkened gap and starts kissing me fiercely while his hands push up under my T-shirt to caress the breasts he's been admiring so openly.

The smoky flavor of his kisses excites me, even as part of me wonders whether this is all just a little too dangerous. The street is quiet, closed off to traffic, but I still worry someone might wander past and spot us. My T-shirt is up almost to my neck now, tits bare and nipples stiffening in the cool of the shadows. Do the police patrol along here, or are they sticking to the main square where pickpockets are likely to lurk? How much trouble might I be in if we were seen?

Then I catch sight of Peter unzipping his shorts, pulling his cock out of his fly. Even limp, it looks big, and my fears of being caught in the act are replaced with the greedy anticipation of having something that size inside me.

While I've been distracted, Gijs has undone my jeans, and his long fingers are burrowing down into my panties. They slither in my juices, seeking out my hole.

"Mmm," he murmurs in my ear. "You've kept yourself nice and tight."

His words encourage me to squeeze hard around his invading digits, demonstrating the extent of my muscle control. But even as he's fingering me with quick in-and-out motions that have me groaning with the depth of my pleasure, I somehow retain the presence of mind to ask, "Who has a condom?"

"I don't," Peter admits.

"I do," Gijs counters.

It means I'll miss out on being fucked by Peter's big cock, but some risks I'm not prepared to take.

While Gijs drops his trousers and rolls on his condom, I sink to my knees. The alley floor is cold and a little uncomfortable, and I'll have the marks of the cobblestones on my skin when I rise, but I figure I won't be down here for too long. That much is obvious when I take the head of Peter's dick between my lips, and he shudders like he's on a short fuse. As I gorge on the juicy plum in my mouth, I tug his foreskin slowly up and down his thick shaft.

"That's it," I hear Gijs mutter, his voice hoarse with lust. "Suck him good. Take his come down your throat."

I can't imagine how sluttish I must look, on my knees in a back alley, half-dressed and with a stranger's cock in my mouth. But I feel powerful, completely in control of Peter's pleasure. While my tongue laves the length of him, my finger rubs at his tight asshole. Playing with that intimate spot is, in my experience, guaranteed to make any man weak at the knees, maybe even anxious to feel that finger burrowing deeper, up into the forbidden recesses of his ass. Peter is no exception. His hands form fists in my hair, trying to pull me harder onto his cock.

But this is going to happen on my terms. I grip his shaft firmly, halfway down its length, so I'm swallowing just as much as I'm comfortable with, and no more.

Peter doesn't argue. He's so close to coming now he barely has the ability to do anything more than give a couple of despairing jerks of his hips. His spunk floods my mouth, thin and carrying the bitter flavor I've come to associate with men who smoke.

He flops back against the wall, and Gijs hauls me without ceremony to my feet. Spinning me around so my palms are flat against the rough brickwork, he gets into position behind me. I feel him guiding himself into me, my juiciness making his entry nice and simple. He gives me the briefest of moments to get used to his size, then he starts to thrust hard while I brace myself with my hands. In the past, I've sometimes been self-conscious of my height, but here, where everyone's so tall, I'm glad of it. Otherwise, this would all be too awkward.

Gijs is just as excited as his friend—and who can blame him, given the show we've just put on for him? He finds my clit, rubbing it as he fucks me. His voice is a rumble in my ear, but he's speaking in Dutch and I can't understand him. Catching a word that sounds familiar, I realize he's asking—or maybe ordering—me to come for him. That won't be difficult. My nerves are taut, sensation building to the point where it threatens to become unbearable. I'm so acutely aware of the fat, latex-sheathed cock buried deep in my cunt, the way it stretches my lips around it as it pulls out almost all the way, then jams back up into me. Control is finally wrested from me by the combination of Gijs's plunging cock and busy finger, and I'm babbling, "Oh, fuck! Oh, Gijs, oh, fuck!" as my orgasm zips through me.

He keeps pounding into me for another few seconds, then he loses it, too. For someone who's made so much noise until now, he does little more than sigh as he comes. My pussy clings on to

him as he pulls out, as if reluctant to let him go. This was even
better than I'd hoped, a nice memory to come back to on nights
when the warmth of summer and the relaxed mood of holiday
time are far away.

When the three of us emerge from the alleyway, we look
respectable, but our flushed faces and a faint aroma of musk must
give the hint something's been happening. The lads return to the
terrace table and their half-finished drinks. I slip back inside,
returning to my wonderful, patient husband, who's ordered me
a fresh drink in my absence. Mike will be so glad I've finally had
the adventure we hoped I would when we originally booked the
holiday. He's not much of a watcher, but he loves to listen, and
he'll adore the tale of my frantic threesome with Peter and Gijs.
And to prove how much I love him, I'm even forgoing my usual
postsex cigarette to share it with him.

BITE ME

Lucy Hughes

Jamie finished his sandwich and licked a bit of mustard off his fingers. "I hate being practically the last one still here."

Lene tossed back the last of her iced tea. "But just think of all the peace and quiet. We could email without anyone standing around looking impatient, take a nap without waking up to people stampeding down the hall, or, you know, whatever we want."

"Right, okay, I'll try to think of it that way." He didn't really intend to, though. He was anxious to move into his new apartment.

She set down her empty bottle and reached across the picnic table to take his hand, which she turned palm up. "Here, let me tell your fortune. I learned how to do this in sixth grade for a library fundraiser."

Jamie let her look at his palm. Any excuse for her to touch him was good, as far as he was concerned. "I thought you said you were shy."

"In some ways." Lene turned his hand a few degrees away from the sun so that the lines were shadowed, and scrutinized it.

While she read his palm, he watched her. Lene's long hippie hair looked almost white in the sunlight. That and her lack of fussy grooming, her utilitarian clothes, and the brisk, purposeful walk were what had first attracted him to her. Here was a girl who only needed a mirror to know she looked great. He'd once said as much to his friend Roger, who replied, "She's a dyke, dumbass."

She traced a finger across his palm. It tickled. "You've got a good strong lifeline. That's supposed to mean you're healthy and energetic. Your head line goes all the way across and even starts to wrap around the side a little down here. Mine does the same thing. It means we analyze things to death."

"You make that sound like a bad thing." He was proud of his ability to consider problems from different angles.

"It's not really good or bad. Now, your fate line is a complete mess." She bit her lip as she considered it. "I don't even know what to make of it. You will live in interesting times, I suppose. Would you relax your hand and let it curl just a little?"

Jamie obliged.

Lene squinted at his hand. "Oh, wow. That's interesting." Her lips moved a tiny bit as she evaluated something.

"What?"

"Your marriage line says you're going to have five children," she said gravely.

Although he didn't really believe in the predictive value of palm reading, that pronouncement distressed him. He tried to tell what part of his hand she was looking at.

Lene looked up at his face with a thoughtful expression, then burst out laughing. "Just kidding. I don't even see a marriage line."

Jamie pulled his hand back. "All right, that's it. No more fortune-telling for you today."

"Oh, come on. Please? I promise I won't make any more things up. I forgot to look at your heart line. That's a major one." She held her hands out to him.

"I already know what it says." He crossed his arms.

She leaned forward, resting her elbows on the table. "What does it say?"

Jamie didn't actually have an answer, let alone a clever one, so he said, "That's classified information."

"And my clearance level isn't high enough, I suppose?" She batted her eyelashes.

He shrugged. "Sorry."

"Hm." She looked over her shoulder with mock furtiveness. "Would you accept a bribe?" she asked in a stage whisper and brushed one of her legs against his under the table.

It took Jamie a moment to process the question and conclude that she was definitely hitting on him. His blood all went south, leaving him dizzy. "Maybe we should discuss this matter somewhere more private, and warmer."

"Indeed. The birds have eyes," she said as she got to her feet. He went with her as soon as he got his wits together enough to remember how his legs worked. When they got a few steps away from the table, a sparrow fluttered down from the roof to pick at their crumbs.

She put her arm around his waist with her hand on his hip, and stopped him for kisses twice before they even made it to the dormitory building. It felt good to be wanted so enthusiastically, though he was kicking himself for not starting anything with her sooner.

As the front door swung shut behind them, Lene stopped him again and leaned into him. He wobbled and braced his shoulder against the sheet of plywood that covered the broken front window. Something sharp jabbed his back near the shoulder blade. She snuggled up to him and kissed his neck and shoulders. Her movements dug the pointy thing into his back harder, and his brain predictably channeled the pain straight into lust.

He concentrated hard to avoid making a sound. It was habit; experience had taught him that if he let a girlfriend know she was hurting him, she would stop, and it would be impossible to persuade her to start again. He tilted his head down to kiss her ravenously. She stood on her toes and her weight shifted. The point against his back broke the skin. He held her close and imagined that she'd done it on purpose.

A moment later, she bounced away from him and launched herself up the stairs, taking them two at a time. He stepped away from the wall and looked back. Three pushpins were stuck into the wood, and a fourth was missing its plastic cap.

"You coming?" Lene called from the second floor.

"Yeah," he said as he started up the stairs.

Her footsteps moved along the hall to his room. How did she know where his room was?

Jamie climbed the stairs slowly, brooding. It was ridiculous that at twenty years old he had to resort to getting his jollies from a defective pushpin. So far, without fail, girls called him weird and accused him of being obsessed if he so much as hinted at what he'd like in bed. He resented it. Most of all, though, he felt starved enough that he was ready to find out whether his feeling about Lene was intuition or wishful thinking.

With determination, but without a plan, he walked down the hall to the room where she was waiting for him on the edge of his bed. She'd taken her sweater off, and the top two buttons of her shirt were undone. The implied invitation registered, but it didn't count yet, in his mind. He meant to sit down next to her, but when he got close enough for her to reach, she wrapped both arms around him and tipped over backward, pulling him down on top of her. He caught himself with his elbows to avoid squashing her.

"Hey, I want you to do me a favor," he said, before he had a chance to lose his nerve.

She said, "Hmm?" and then waited quietly while he tugged his shirt off. Her hands settled on his back again, cool against his skin. "Ooh, you're warm."

"Bite me." He offered her the inside of his left arm.

She looked bemused, but caught a bit of skin between her teeth and toyed with it gently.

In the pit of his stomach, a host of little demons readied a vat of despair in case he needed to wallow in it. "Like you mean it," he added with forced optimism.

That got her to apply a little more pressure. It felt slightly pinchy.

"Harder?" He wanted her to make him scream.

A little more pressure. The tiny increments were driving him crazy. He clenched his teeth, as though that could make her bite down harder.

"Like you're a vampire who's been starving for a week," he suggested.

She let go. "Herbivore teeth. Not made to draw blood."

"I know, but it'll hurt like hell," he told her, desperately willing her to understand.

She looked into his eyes. He wished he could read her expression, but for several long seconds, all he could see was his own reflection. He held his breath and his heartbeat filled his chest. "Are you okay?" he asked when he couldn't take the silence anymore.

"Yes," she said.

He couldn't tell if she meant it. "Then talk to me. Say something."

"I've never had any inclination in that direction."

He rolled off of her and flopped on his back. "Story of my life." He didn't care if he sounded bitter. What was so hard about hurting a guy? You'd think he was asking for someone to bite the head off a kitten.

"I know, but it'll hurt like hell," Jamie said. He was staring at Lene too intently for someone just asking for a simple favor. Just fantastic—she finally had him half naked in bed after daydreaming about him for months, and he was springing a fetish on her that she didn't understand. It was like one of those moments in a movie where something goes wrong and the grand swell of music grinds to a halt.

Lene ran through a few choice swear words in her head, but kept her mouth shut. She didn't want to say something rash and hurt his feelings before she had time to process the information.

"Are you okay?" he prompted.

"Yes," she said.

"Then talk to me. Say something."

She tried to think of the most neutral way to say it. "I've never had any inclination in that direction."

He rolled off of her and flopped on his back dramatically enough to bounce. "Story of my life," he grumbled.

So much for not saying the wrong thing. She turned onto her side and propped her head on her hand. "I'm not saying I won't do it." Mom used to say, *You don't know you don't like something unless you've tried it*. Granted, the advice was dispensed in the context of casseroles and green vegetables, but it generalized well. One bite was the least she could do.

"Oh." His face relaxed.

"But you threw me a little." She stroked his short dark hair. "And tell me if I'm wrong, but the way you were looking at me, I got the feeling that you wanted more than one little thing."

He closed his eyes. "Sorry. I thought you might like to bite, but really, it's just that I like pain with sex. Or messing around or whatever it is that we're doing. There never seems to be a good time to mention this."

"So you're a masochist," she said.

He winced, squeezing his eyes shut tighter for a moment. "Technically, but I hate the word. The guy it's named after was an asshole to his wife and wrote a really bad book."

"I didn't know." She let her hand slide down from his hair to his chest, and finally hooked a finger through one of his belt loops. He might ask for odd things, but that didn't interfere with her desire to tear the rest of his clothes off and run her hands and her tongue all over his beautiful mocha skin. "So give me some idea of the scale here. Do you want a little nibble here and there or..."

"Whatever you're comfortable with."

"I was taking that for granted. I just want to know what you want so I can see if I'm comfortable with it." She was starting to feel annoyed with him. If she was going to be a good sport and humor him, making it simple and explaining exactly what he wanted was the least he could do.

"Anything short of permanent damage is all good. At least I think it is. I haven't had much chance to find out." He bit his lip.

Lene suspected that he was wrong. She thought of three probable exceptions in as many seconds: Hundreds of paper cuts. Being stung by a Portuguese man o' war. A bad hangover. "That's awfully open ended. Don't people usually spell it out a little more?" She tugged on his belt loop and inched a little closer. She had a few specific ideas about what *she* wanted, at least.

"I'm not people, and this isn't usually. I don't have a laundry list of kinks."

"This is surreal enough already, I'm not a telepath, and you're being about as helpful as a hookah-smoking caterpillar."

His response was a flippant, "Bite me."

In a moment of pique, she actually did feel like hurting him, so she found the faint imprint of her teeth on the inside of his upper arm and bit fiercely. The visceral jolt inside her when he drew a short, sharp breath and tensed up startled her. His eyes were open when she looked up. "That good?" She halfway expected him to say no.

He pulled her on top of him and wrapped her in a full-body hug. "Very," he whispered. His skin was warm and soft against her cheek. He seemed so happy about her biting him that her irritation vanished like a snowflake in a mug of hot chocolate.

"Okay. Let me try again." She turned her head and nipped at his other arm. His hands pressed harder against her back and he squirmed under her. She clamped her teeth down slowly, taking time to taste his reaction and hers. At first, he relaxed a little bit and stroked her back, making little contented sounds, but gradually shifted to a more conventional response to pain. When he arched his back, squeezed her and tightened his throat to keep from yelling, a rush of elation poured into her body through the heart. It would have taken her breath away if he hadn't already been squeezing her so hard she could barely breathe.

When she let go, they both took a few seconds to catch up on oxygen. Lene wondered what neurotransmitters and hormones went into the experience. It felt too good to be straight-up epinephrine. She cut that train of thought off sharply, with a promise to deconstruct later. "Curiouser and curiouser."

"Is that good?" he asked, with an audible smile. He slid his hands down her back to her bum and made sure she knew just how good it was for him by grinding against her.

"Ah...yeah, I think so." A few bites later, she was sure of it. Impulses to cover him with kisses or marks from her teeth whirled around her brain until she couldn't tell one from the other. The guilt and pity that she'd been expecting never materialized. Feeling him struggle with himself to hold still for her and keep quiet made her hungrier. It was an irresistible dare, challenging her to break that control.

Lene scooted down and found a place on his side under his rib cage that looked vulnerable. She nuzzled the spot and kissed it. He gripped her shoulder with nervous fingers. She chomped down with abandon. He yelped and threw her off the bed. She knocked over a couple of packed cardboard moving boxes on her way down, mashing one of them significantly with her head.

Jamie scrambled to the edge of the bed and looked down at her, wide-eyed. "Sorry! You all right?"

She lay on her back on the rug with her arms out at her sides, grinning like an idiot. She could feel the place where her head collided with the box, but it wasn't serious. "Yep. You?"

"Just reflexes. Sorry. I didn't mean to hurt you."

Lene peeled herself off the floor and stood. "Don't worry about it. I'm going to hurt you a lot more."

He laughed. "Well, that was quick. I thought you said you never had any inclination in this direction."

"That was over five minutes ago. Ancient history. Why are we still wearing clothes?"

Jamie shrugged and lay back down. She unbuttoned her shirt the rest of the way. He unfastened his belt, raised his hips a little, and slid it out of the belt loops. He offered it to her. She took it, and understood why he'd been vague; this would have gone over poorly five minutes ago.

He kicked his shoes onto the floor. "If you've had enough concussions for one day, there's duct tape in the box we just dented."

She yanked the box, marked MISC, opened it without a second thought and rummaged carelessly through the clutter of toiletries and desk supplies for a few seconds until she came up with tape. Presumably he'd forgive her for spilling all his paper-clips. When she turned around, he was unbuttoning his jeans, a pleasure that she wanted for herself. He hesitated when he saw her slight frown.

Lene came back to bed wearing the roll of duct tape as a bracelet. She set down the belt and pushed his hands up over his head, pinning them at the wrists, possessive. He looked absurdly sexy wearing the bruises she'd given him, and ready for more. "Are you sure you're up for anything short of permanent damage? Once I get you taped up, I want to take a lot of liberties with you."

He hesitated before he said yes. She heard the timber of fear in his voice, and her heart beat faster. Although she still didn't entirely believe him, she believed that his yes covered anything she was likely to actually do. "Good. Hold still a sec." She found the end of the tape, unrolled a long strip and tore it off with her teeth.

Instead of holding still, he reached around and unhooked her bra while she was busy with the tape, and cupped her breasts with his hands. When she looked down at him and raised her eyebrows, he said, "I thought I'd take a couple liberties with you while I can." He pinched her nipples lightly, then placed his hands back where she'd left them. That was the last coherent thing he said for some time.

* * *

Lene rolled Jamie onto his back again, with his cooperation. She was getting efficient with the tape, and quickly had his feet secured to the footboard, keeping his legs apart. His arms ached from being bound in the same position for however many minutes or hours it had been.

"Anything I need to know before I gag you?" she asked, holding up a small strip of tape.

He shook his head no. He was dimly aware of a number of things that would be smart to say, but he didn't feel like talking.

She covered his mouth and kissed him through the tape, then drew back and regarded him with a satisfied smile. Her fingernails left pink trails of heat as she dragged them from his collarbone to his thigh.

Pain didn't have the same edge it did when they'd started. He basked in it instead of struggling to get away and tried to ask her for more with his eyes.

Lene obliged him for a minute, raking fire up and down his body, but then caught sight of something and paused. She touched her finger to his forearm, and showed him the drop of blood on her fingertip. He closed his eyes and shuddered. She drew her wet finger across his cheek slowly.

"I didn't mean to do that, but if you could see yourself right now..." She sighed and turned his head to the side, with his bloody cheek facing up. "You look lovely in red."

It felt right. After all she'd put him through, after he'd buried his face in the pillow and yelled until his throat hurt along with everything else, it would have been odd if he hadn't bled. He opened his eyes a sliver when she stood up from the bed.

She crouched over the open moving box rummaging through his things again, and came back holding a fresh razor blade.

He stared. That was one of the things he'd thought vaguely
of asking her not to do, and now he couldn't. She was going to
cut him, and there was nothing he could do or say to stop her.
Once that sank in, he accepted it. He'd be still so she wouldn't
cut too deep by mistake.

Lene set the razor blade down carefully on his chest. She
straddled him and unzipped her pants. "I'm thinking about
what I'm going to do to you in a minute." She slid a hand under
her purple underwear and touched herself quietly for a minute,
watching him—mostly his face.

It excited him to know that she was getting off on the idea
of making him bleed for her, and having his hands bound was
frustrating. He tried to rub against her, but she didn't allow it
much—just enough to drive him even more crazy.

She closed her eyes for a moment, then relaxed with a shiver
and withdrew her hand.

Jamie was still very much aware of the razor blade sitting on
his chest, waiting.

But first, she decided to go down on him. Her hand and her
mouth were both so warm and friendly after all that teasing.
She put her whole body into it, rubbing against his leg and
rolling her shoulders in time with her tongue until he knew it
was going to put him over the edge if she didn't stop. Girls liked
a little warning, didn't they? He tried his best to communicate
in muffled squeaks. She intensified her efforts, and he had no
choice but to come, even if it meant she'd pick up the razor
blade that much sooner, or possibly because of it. Gravity took
a holiday, and the world dissolved into pure white bliss.

Awash with tingly satisfaction, he couldn't have moved even
if his limbs were free. Lene kissed him repeatedly, moving up his
stomach and chest until she got to the razor blade. She paused
dramatically, picked it up and turned it over in her fingers.

He stopped breathing. *Don't do it. Not now.*

She tossed the blade back into the box it had come out of and grinned. "Psych."

The late afternoon sun angled through the window, illuminating dust motes and casting a bright golden square against the back of the door. Jamie and Lene lounged against a pile of pillows, sheets, bits of tape, and jumbled clothes, after-glowing.

"I'm afraid this may be habit forming," she said.

Jamie used his toes to retrieve the blanket from the floor. "Thank god." His voice was strained. He shivered and pulled the blanket over both of them. "It feels like I lost my virginity all over again."

Lene snuggled up to him to warm him up. "I don't know how to explain what I feel like, but it's really good." It was sort of true. She was madly in love, and no longer able to convince herself otherwise. The idea of saying so aloud just then terrified her and would probably scare him off, too.

They cuddled quietly for a minute before Lene realized from the change in his breathing that Jamie had fallen asleep. She eased out of the bed an inch at a time to avoid waking him, and put her shirt back on. While she brushed the tangles out of her hair with her fingers, she inspected his face one more time to make sure she hadn't left any handprints. No bruises were coming up on his cheek—pretty good for not having a clue what she was doing. She resisted the urge to kiss his face. There was no need to wake him yet.

Instead, she performed a few ballet steps in the sunbeam, then hunted quietly through the box of "misc" for antibiotic goop and a Band-Aid.

RIDE A
COWBOY

Del Carmen

I want to fuck you."

Rita didn't know who was more surprised. She, at the words that came out of her mouth, or Nate, who looked at her like a steer caught in headlights.

"What?" he asked.

Rita pretended the last minute hadn't happened. She waved her pad at him. "What would you like to order?"

Nate lifted an eyebrow, a knowing look in his eyes.

She steeled herself. Hopefully whatever cut he gave her would not be loud enough for the other diners to hear. The last thing she needed or wanted was the town gossip mill looking in her direction.

"I'll take the blue-plate special," he said, "the steak medium well, heavy on the gravy, four biscuits. Coffee. Black."

Rita wrote furiously and reached for his menu.

He held on to it and forced her to meet his eyes, his questioning, hers resolved.

He let go of the menu. Rita forced herself to walk slowly

toward the kitchen, all the while yearning to run from the room. She put in the order and kept walking down the hallway, out the back door. Leaning on the wall, she took deep breaths to calm her racing heart and covered her face with her hands. She shook her head and dried her sweaty palms on her apron, a blush hot on her cheeks.

Stupid. Stupid. Stupid. She couldn't believe she had given voice to her secret obsession, and to Nate's face, no less. She wouldn't have been surprised if he had leapt onto his horse and ridden for the hills.

But he looked so hot in his tight jeans, and whenever he wore his white shirt and leather vest combo, all she could think of was riding a cowboy—Nate, to be exact. She'd ride him until he was wild and sweaty, until she'd quenched her lust for him.

Rita heard her name being called. She straightened her hair, her Mexican lace blouse and her spine as she entered the diner.

Nate's eyes followed her, as she filled coffee cups, took food requests and chatted with her customers. Aside from refilling his cup, Rita ignored him. On any other day, she would have rejoiced at having him linger over his meal so she could steal glances at his chiseled features, his dark wavy hair, and the big bulge in his jeans. She'd built fantasies around him and that bulge. Her favorite was the one of them fucking in a booth, ending with his tongue on her clit and his cock in her mouth. On any other day—but not today. She wanted him to leave so she could soak her head.

Rita put the check upside down in front of Nate and quickly stacked the dishes. "I'll get these out of your way." She was talking too fast, a clear sign of nervousness.

Nate caught her hand. She froze.

"Is there something else you want?" she asked, not meeting his eyes.

"You." He ran his fingers across her skin.

"What?" Did she just squeak?

"You." His voice was confident and strong. "Your breasts cupped in my hands, my tongue in your mouth, my dick..."

Rita pressed her fingers against his mouth and looked around frantically in case anyone had heard.

He pulled one of her fingers into the dark wetness of his mouth. Her eyes looked into his. Hunger stared back. She saw his eyes drop to her breasts. She imagined him sucking her nipples and desire pooled in her cunt.

For a second, they were alone with their desires; only the tinkling of china brought them back to reality. He let her pull her finger free, but she couldn't resist stroking his lips.

"What time do you get off?" His hand was still hot on hers.

"I'm closing tonight." Her voice was breathless.

"I'll be back to fuck you then." He stood in one smooth movement. The heat of his body was intoxicating as it pressed against her briefly. The warmth of his breath caressed her neck and sent shivers down her body.

Rita took the plates and headed toward the kitchen. She watched Nate walk out the door. He had a tight ass and a swagger. Very John Wayne. Very sexy. She looked at the large clock over the counter: two hours to closing.

Closing time crawled closer. Customers came and went. The kitchen closed. Rita was finally alone. She pushed tables and chairs around, preparing the diner for a private seductive encounter.

Her panties were damp with lust.

Maybe he wouldn't come. Doubt plagued her, but she pushed it away. *He'll come,* she told herself. *He'll come, in more ways than one.* A smile touched her lips.

Candles, she thought. They needed candles. Rita ran into

the kitchen and grabbed a handful and some matches. She had just finished lighting the last one when she sensed the man at the door.

His silhouette screamed cowboy: hat, vest, tight jeans, bulge.

"Say it again," he asked.

"I want to fuck you." She trembled as he crossed to her.

The room was dark, except from the soft candlelight and the glare coming from the kitchen window. Rita took in Nate's handsome features, the hunger naked on his face. Never had she craved a man more.

He tossed his hat onto one of the booths and reached for her. His mouth was hot and wet on hers, his dick hard against her belly.

"I want to be balls deep in you already." Big hands cupped her breasts. She had taken off her bra earlier so the lace from her blouse was rough against the sensitive peaks. She almost came when he sucked her nipples through the lace.

He caught her moan with his mouth. His tongue demanded entrance and was welcomed.

She was his for the taking and he took. He pulled her skirt and panties down in one move, and boldly slid his fingers over her swollen clit and wet pussy. He inserted a finger, then two. She bucked against them and grabbed on to him for fear of falling.

His shoulders were hard beneath her fingers, warm against her palms. She opened his shirt, sculpting and rubbing his chest. She couldn't resist pressing her nose to his throat. He smelled of horses, grass and manly sweat.

She heard his intake of breath. His hands were rough on her hair as he pulled her lips to meet his. He devoured her, his lips sucking and licking. He tasted of pure ambrosia. Suddenly, he released her and removed the rest of their clothes.

Her naked cowboy was built: wide chest, fine muscles, strong thighs and a big dick. Her hand couldn't close completely around his thickness.

She knelt in front of him and ran her hand up and down his shaft. It was a beautiful thing—long, thick, hard and pointing straight at her. She rubbed her face—cheeks, nose, lips—against his sex. She swirled her tongue down his length, tasting the muskiness. She licked the drop of come on the tip of his penis and took him into her mouth, opening wider, and wider still, to accommodate his size.

Rita felt his hands in her hair as he thrust his dick deeper into her mouth, until the tip of his penis touched the back of her throat. She grazed him with her teeth. She could do this all night, she thought, and continued sucking harder, fucking faster. Her mouth moved up and down his cock.

He pulled out of her with a small popping sound.

"I want to be inside you first." His voice growled with lust as he pulled her up. Taking a quick look around, he grabbed his pants and headed for the back booth she had prepared.

He sat and she mounted herself a naked cowboy, her cunt rubbing against his hard penis.

She laughed as he pulled a strip of condoms from his pocket.

"I have more if we run out," she whispered against his lips.

The condom was rolled on quickly and she seated herself fully on his cock. His hands anchored her on his lap. She threw her head back, her body arching, as her cunt stretched to accommodate his thickness, stretched to suck all of him in.

She rocked slowly at first, looking for a good rhythm. She took him in as deeply as she could with each downward thrust. He thrust upward, again and again. Their ride was fast and furious.

She rode her cowboy long and hard. His thrusts escalated, giving neither one relief. Hunger and need drove them, until the only sounds in the room were their moans and the soft slap of their heated sweaty bodies coming together.

She could feel the pressure rising within her. The hurting was so good and suddenly too much.

He grabbed her hips; his calloused fingers pressed into her heated flesh. He brought her down until he was balls deep inside her. He thrust deep one last time and her orgasm burst open. Her whole body shuddered with pure pleasure. She heard his shout echo throughout the room.

They collapsed into each other's arms. He buried his face between her breasts; her head rested on top of his. They clung together as the aftermath of their passion rumbled inside them. Her hands were around his torso, his around her waist. Delicious shivers danced on their skin.

She felt a gentle tug at her breast. She sat back against his thighs, but tightened the lips of her vagina to keep him inside her. Their eyes and then their mouths met.

"I love the service here." His voice was husky from their shared passion. "I'll have to come more often."

"You will," she promised.

Their laughter was soft and intimate and just the beginning, for they had all night to explore each other and the many surfaces of the diner. She was looking forward to riding her cowboy into the sunrise.

QUEEN
OF SHEBA

Jen Cross

You really wanna know about the best time? Well, there was this one guy, back when I was in school. But you have to promise you won't tell Max. Okay?

At first, I thought Jimmy was just really into foreplay. He'd say, "Can I touch you?" And before I was done nodding, he'd have reached out a calloused hand to my body, maybe resting it on one of my thighs or against my belly for a second, but he was always only interested in my pussy. His eyes would glaze a little, he'd moisten his lips and get focused like a cat.

When Jimmy really got going, my pussy would feel like it was molten, you know? All melty and hot, like—well, I'm getting ahead of myself here.

Jimmy, with that mouth and tongue, those lips. He'd push up every single pillow behind me and set me back against them, prop my feet up and over to either side of my mussed single bed. After he'd sort of enthroned me, got my butt and hips propped up and thighs splayed, he'd just sit back for a minute and look at me, those ruddy cheeks flushing and his eyes bright and almost—if it weren't for the cocky set to his jaw, the way his grin pulled a little too tight to one side of his mouth so you'd never be sure he wasn't about to crack up—*almost* reverent.

He never did, though—never cracked up, never laughed at me. He just liked to keep me perched on that edge of nerves. But really, maybe I just couldn't read him, after all those months, and there was something else altogether going on behind those eyes and that half-cracked grin.

I can't even remember exactly when or how we met. We were both scholarship students at a school full of kids whose parents had been planning for their darling Jacks' and Janes' educations since the moment of conception. I do remember him coming to meet a study partner of mine who was in one of the huge survey classes I was drowning in. I'll never know what it was he saw in me and we never were much for talking, but a few nights later, Jimmy showed up at my door with pizza and a couple of Dr. Peppers and a small bundle of flowers that he'd picked on his way over, snatching them from one of the university's landscaped gardens. I was charmed—and a pretty horny and somewhat easy lay. Thank goodness.

He'd look at me for so long that I'd start to cover myself some-times—the staring was so unusual and here I was, a girl who hadn't been much for nudity, even if no one else was around. In high school, I'd been one of those girls dressing in the bathroom stalls for gym for the first two years, till my friend Jackson, you remember him, pointed out one day that I had bigger tits than most of the girls in my class, and that if anyone said anything it'd be out of pure jealousy. I didn't exactly believe him, but I risked changing by my locker finally and except for a wisecracked,

"Well, shit, look who's finally joining us out here," there were no other comments. I mean, what was I even expecting?

Except maybe the way my mom used to cut her eyes at me when I'd be getting ready for school in the morning, wondering why I bothered with doing my hair or putting any color to my lips—looking at me like I thought I was the Queen of Sheba, when I was really such a cow.

With Jimmy, there was something else going on. He'd look at me like I was beautiful, the way someone pauses, kind of dumbstruck, before a stunning work of art or a breathtaking sunrise, stops to really be present with that spiderweb caught with morning dew stuck up there between the peeling paint and cracked window frame of your first apartment—you know. I mean, the only person who'd ever told me they thought I was beautiful was my dad, and that was when he wanted me to let him watch me in the shower. And then, in high school, if some guy liked you, you knew that as soon as he told you how pretty he thought you were, you'd hear him joking about you with his friends. I used to hate that feeling, how the big openness of longing and being longed for got dropped, reverted back into a kind of pit of loss and shame and embarrassment; when I realized that maybe they were just kidding after all—do you know what I mean?

But things with Jimmy were strange and different, and of course, he was hard to believe. When I tried to cover myself, he used to just say, "Wait—please, Steph," and even though I'd keep my hand on the sheets, I wouldn't pull them up over me, over my curves, the pushes of flesh around my belly, the little hairs darkening my thighs, or, sure, the split of my pussy or my breasts. Over the months we were involved, I got more comfortable, even sometimes spreading myself wider for him, more open—like I deserved to be so displayed, like I was exquisite, unique.

Sometimes he'd touch himself while he looked, his cock hardening behind the fabric of his boxers and khakis with its preternatural twitching, and I would clench inside myself, feel the rose blush spread from my chest.

Don't tell me you don't know what it was. I knew. But still, I loved it.

He'd brush his fingers through my thick pubic curls, loosening the free hairs, and then he'd bend forward, dive in. His body would sort of fold. He wanted inside me and sure I know that as a whole person, I didn't exactly exist anymore when he got into that wet fleshy focus, but at the same time I knew in that moment that I was being revered.

Now, like I said, I had reason in my life to believe that my body would never be reverenced, so when he put his mouth on me that way the very first time, when his throat opened and his warm, damp breath eased and heated across my pussy, propped up and open as I was in my little chilly dorm room, I just about started to cry. I mean, the wet prickled all around my eyes and my nose started to run. When I sniffled, Jimmy raised his eyes up to me sharply, not exactly in surprise, but not exactly knowing either. He just smiled, pulled one hand off my thigh and caressed my cheek.

"You are *so* beautiful, Stephanie—"

And this is what happened in my head: now, I know that I am supposed to be a self-actualized woman, and it doesn't matter, or shouldn't, whether a man wants me or not or thinks I'm cute and yes, I know, I'm smart and believe in the power of reasonable footwear and warm clothes in bad weather and I was raised on feminism and will never disavow my own inner strength, but—and it kills me that this has turned out to be true—I got so wet when he said that to me, so thick and soft and open, so scared that maybe he didn't really mean it and, oh, I just wanted to quit thinking so much and feel what he was about to do.

Jimmy helped me with that right away, dropping his head back down between my thighs and letting his tongue smooth slow and wide up from the bottom of my pussy to my clit, and I gasped and let my legs fall farther open, which was nearly impossible. He'd ripple his tongue up across me, never exactly settling in any one spot but instead touching my whole pussy, all at once. Then he'd focus back in, suckling hard and fast, with such a quick change that I'd see stars and start to beat the bed.

My hips got good and stretched that season with Jimmy— he could spend a whole lot of time between my legs. At first, thinking he was just really into foreplay, like I said, I figured he'd give my pussy the same few licks and half suckle that my other boyfriends had offered, anxiously humping the mattress in anticipation of the real thing. But no. Jimmy languished there, lavished attention, bathed me in sensation and pleasure, built a kind of longing I hadn't known before—and, frankly, haven't known since. Now, that's just between us.

Jimmy would use his hands to hold me open, and his whole mouth, his nose and chin and cheeks. He'd fuck me with his tongue, then lap at me with the full flat of it, wriggle the tip across my clit, then capture the fat little head between his thin lips and suckle first gently, then more sharply, as I came. And came. And came.

He got me off so many times when he was down there, like that was the whole point. Can you imagine? He may have come in his hand or his pants sometimes—I never really knew; I was too busy screaming and lost in the pillows, grabbing his head, shoving my hips up into his face, sometimes capturing my tits in my own hands (if I wanted any other part of my body to get some attention, I had to give it myself; Jimmy was nothing if not focused).

I felt gluttonous, fat and lazy and joyful, those few months—like I had something someone could gorge himself on, and yet *I* came out the other side deeply satiated.

I offered to return the favor, though I was terrified he might accept; I'd always gagged on boyfriends' cocks in the past, and I couldn't keep it up for very long in those days. But Jimmy dismissed my offering, not as ridiculous, exactly—more like something sweet but silly, like how your folks smile at you when you tell them you're going to build them a big house on the moon someday.

He just urged me to settle back and set himself to slowly licking again, practically feeding, and I would close my eyes and forget that any other kind of sex existed.

And even though things came to a near-screeching halt when, first, Jimmy called me *Meredith* while his tongue was buried thick between my pussy lips, and *then* when my coworker Brenda started describing this great guy she was seeing, who ate her pussy for hours and made her feel more beautiful than she had ever imagined feeling. Jimmy changed something in me, opened me up to my body in ways I hadn't imagined before he set me up on a throne of my own pillows, gently pushed my legs apart and told me, before bending down at the waist so I could watch his broad back and light curly hair descend onto me, "My god, Stephanie—you are *so* pretty."

I get worked up about it even now—just look at my hands shaking. He wanted to make all the girls feel beautiful, I guess. After Brenda, I didn't return Jimmy's calls anymore, didn't open the door for him when he came over. He left two messages on my answering machine, though: the first one was so dirty that I erased it before he was halfway through describing what he wanted to make a date with me to do, and the second was so simple: "Please let me see you, Stephanie. I miss how you taste." It was so honest; I don't mind telling you, I got all wet just hearing those words. Maybe it was a mistake to pick my pride—or my self-respect, I'm not sure which it was—over the magic of his mouth. But what's done is done, of course. And Max and I have a fine time together. Nobody wants to be the Queen of Sheba all the time in bed anyway, does she?

HOT FOR TEACHER

Rachel Kramer Bussel

M eredith straightened her skirt, settled herself beneath her desk with her crisp new notebook and set of her favorite black pens before her, feeling, in many ways, like she was back in high school, with all her nervousness about her outfit, teachers and what her classmates would think of her. Whereas some of her peers could barely remember what they'd done last week, memory wasn't a problem for Meredith; in fact, a surfeit of memory might have been her main problem. She couldn't stop herself from replaying the same old daunting images, and when she should have been paying attention to the equations being written on the board, all she could think about was the fact that Professor Arthur reminded her, in style if not in looks, of her very first real boyfriend, Geoff, in college the first time around, the one she'd given her virginity to, the one she'd thought would be forever. He'd also been adorably nerdy, jittery and hopped up on coffee and optimism. She shook her head to clear it of the memory of him sliding off her panties under their picnic blanket

and getting her off while their friends sailed Frisbees and kicked
soccer balls around them.

Meredith fiddled with the simple turquoise and silver ring
she'd bought to cover the deep grooves on her fourth finger, the
one she'd worn her wedding ring on since that first time around
in college, after Geoff, when she'd decided it was time to get
serious—right after she'd found out she was pregnant. It was a
groove she feared would be forever etched into her skin, the way
those pesky memories seemed to play on permanent repeat in
her mind. She looked around the room at the kids young enough
to be her sons and daughters, some of them younger than her
actual son and daughter, with only a handful in their later twenties and thirties. She was forty-two, solidly middle-aged, and
determined to get her bachelor's degree and reclaim some of the
youth she'd lost when she stepped away from academia to go
on the road with her sexy new band member boyfriend-turned-
husband. Following Clay had seemed like the right thing to do;
she didn't want to be one of those women who sat around all day
and complained about every pregnancy ache and pain. Instead,
she'd watched show after show, then after party upon after
party, where Clay had proceeded to flirt with every girl who
walked by, as if she were nothing more than another groupie.
Eventually, but only after giving birth twice, Meredith realized
that's exactly what she was. They'd tried to make it work, with
Clay setting up an in-home studio, but the kids had been little
when they'd finally called it quits.

She'd worked a series of office jobs, but after this latest round
of layoffs, she knew something had to change. She'd never given
herself permission to chase her dream, but with the severance,
and both her kids out of the house, she knew she had to do
something for herself or she'd go mad. Meredith soon realized
that there were other dreams she'd neglected over the years, too;

other needs she'd figured were for younger, hotter women. Who had time to get her hair done, to dress up, when she was working sixty-hour weeks? Men had asked her out and she'd even taken one or two up on their offers of overnight visits, quick rolls in the hay that did little more than stoke her passion and make her wistful for what might have been.

The sad truth was that she couldn't remember being as raw, as wet, as wanton as when she'd been with Clay. Until now. Her professor was far from a Clay-like bad boy, but still, he did something to her that made her want to either be the best student he'd ever seen, or the worst, if it meant detention and the chance to get properly punished. She bit her lip as a highly irrelevant, not to mention irreverent, giggle threatened to burst from her lips as she pictured herself in a schoolgirl skirt, white cotton panties, white kneesocks and pigtails with red ribbons. It was not an outfit she'd ever come close to wearing, and that's why it appealed to her. She'd never had a chance to play at being a bad girl, to try on that persona or any other besides young mom, really, followed by older and now middle-aged mom.

She was the oldest student in the class, and as such, was supposed to be some kind of role model. She could tell by the way the others gave her a wide berth, smiling politely at her but otherwise treating her as if age itself were contagious, or like she was going to tattle on them for misbehaving when the last thing she cared about was their grades or potential offenses. The others could spend all of class texting and flirting and passing notes, but Meredith, even if she didn't understand every concept, wanted points for paying attention, for disrupting her previously boring but safe life to perk up her mind. She hadn't known her pussy was going to follow along as easily.

Professor Arthur was writing on the board with his back turned to the class, so she could properly peruse him. He, too, was young enough to be her son, if she'd had kids even earlier than she had. From the back, he looked like an average white guy, sandy blond hair, blue and white button-down, jeans, brown loafers. He hadn't said much more than hello and that he was about to teach them Economics 101. Meredith had her own kind of economic knowledge, gleaned from not only balancing the family budget and grocery shopping and watching her meager bank account and 401(k) grow at a snail's pace, but also from seeing her preteen daughter grasp on to fashion trends the moment she read about them in one of her magazines. Meredith barely remembered what it had been like to be that young, though sitting in this seat brought memories rushing back, like passing notes with her best friend Jenny as they discussed whether Billy Tilson liked either of them and if Mrs. Singer's glamorous hair was natural or dyed and if they'd be allowed to go to the Jewish youth group sleepover.

Later, they'd talked about how they hated their moms and wanted to run away and who'd buy them drinks. Now, she'd been through the cycle of being the mom her teens pretended to hate, then the one who missed them fiercely. She could feel everyone staring at her and didn't know where to look, so she examined her French manicure, the same style she'd been getting every week for the last ten years. Maybe it was time for a change, she mused, as she looked at the girls with blue and magenta and multicolored nails.

There was only so much changing she could do, though, and right now she just wanted to make sure she passed all her classes. Getting A's would be nice, but the degree was what she was after. She had worked too hard for too long, plus all those years where her mind had felt like it was going bad, like fruit left out for too long, softening into mush as she struggled to keep one foot in that world, picking up a weighty classic now and then, its tiny print and heady ideas making her struggle in the best kind of way. Finally, the bell rang and she stood up in a daze.

She found herself wandering up to the front of the classroom, her feet moving before her mind could fully process what she was doing. "Hi, Professor," she started.

"Call me Ralph," he said.

"Ralph," she began again. "I just wanted to say that I like your teaching style. I still don't totally understand everything we're doing in here; I don't have much of a business sense, but I am excited to be learning. In the back of my mind I have an idea for running my own bakery and..." She trailed off, not really sure what she wanted other than to bask in his nearness.

He turned and beamed his full attention, not to mention two rows of extremely even white teeth, right at her. "If you ever have any questions, Meredith, you are more than welcome to visit me in my office during office hours. It's totally confidential," he said, and she wondered if she was imagining that his voice got low and intimate somehow on that last word. Were they still talking about homework?

"I think that might be helpful," she said, meaning, in fact, *I'd love to dress up for you and bend over your desk.* "Well, I'll see you soon," she said.

"I hope so," he said quietly, unless she'd imagined that too.

She went home and for the first time in who knows how long, she stripped down to her birthday suit and simply walked around every room enjoying the feel of the air against her bare skin. She took baths, of course, and even got massages, but those were merely utilitarian reasons for nudity. This afternoon was about her picturing herself prancing around for Professor Arthur, showing him her pendulous, large breasts, her sizeable ass, the curve of her belly, the dusting of red fuzz covering her

pussy. She dyed her hair a very shiny brown, trying to fool the
world into thinking her a brunette, but inside her lurked the
soul of a redhead, one whose innate passion had been put on
hold for far too long. Instead of taking a bath, Meredith stood
in her bathroom and began touching herself the way she wanted
Professor Arthur—"Ralph," she said aloud to herself—to touch
her. She began with her breasts, tweaking each one, holding up
the nipples and tugging and twisting until the sight caused a
corresponding tug in her pussy.

Then, staring at herself in the mirror, Meredith lifted her
right breast and tucked her head down so she could suck on her
own nipple. The flood of emotion and arousal was so intense
she had to lean her left hand against the counter. She spread her
legs, wondering if Professor Arthur was circumcised, picturing
his cock as big and thick and aching just for her. She kept going,
making sure to watch her every move, so that when she did
go to her hot professor's office hours, it wouldn't be as a true
schoolgirl, skittish and nervous, relying on her youthful charm
and giggly giddiness, but as a mature woman who could tap
into that spirit, but also had something more to offer. For all her
pleated-skirt fantasies, what Meredith wanted was to be treated
like a woman—a woman who knew exactly what she wanted,
even if what she wanted was to be manhandled by a younger
nerdy man who just so happened to hold her academic future
in his hands.

She searched her closet, determined to find something there
capable of seduction. She could afford to shop, at least a little,
but Meredith wanted something familiar, a reminder that
even in all these years when dating had taken a backseat to
the mundane truths of Real Life and mothering, she'd remembered the girl who threw her bra onstage and got fingered back-
stage, who was wet and wild and carefree. She rummaged and

rummaged and finally, in the back of the closet, found a red and purple dress she vaguely remembered buying, if not wearing. There were no tags on it, but the purple silk outlining the red shimmery fabric made her smile. She immediately shucked off her T-shirt and jeans and slipped it over her head, seeing that she'd need a new bra, one to be worn strategically peeking out from beneath this dress's straps.

She turned sideways, admiring the way the dress clung to her breasts, proud of them, proud of herself for not having even considered having them lifted or added to, the way so many of the women she knew had done. Meredith cupped her hands over her breasts, letting her nipples peek out, hoping Professor Arthur would like her in this dress, like her as more than a student. She decided maybe she didn't need a bra, after all—or panties. If she was going to go for it, she was going to go for it.

She hadn't really caught all of what he'd been talking about, but the basic lesson of supply and demand was one Meredith understood. The question was, were there other suppliers of the kind of quick, hot, dirty sex she was offering? Of course, there was only one of her, but would he be able to see exactly what she wanted, what she was demanding as well as supplying? Meredith lifted her dress and examined her pussy, the boldness of the act making her blush. Maybe there was a bit of a school-girl in her.

She dusted powder and blush onto her cheeks, borrowed a leftover black glittery eyeliner her daughter had left lying around the bathroom to widen her brown eyes, tossed her hair and added a soft pink hue to her lips, followed by gloss. She didn't know what the look she was going for said, but she definitely looked a far cry from her classroom persona. There, she was all about learning, absorbing, letting him run the show. By now, she was so needy, she was ready to take what she was looking for. Not without his consent, of course, that was never her plan, but if he wanted her to make the first move, she would. She could play the older woman, even if she wasn't sure that's what this was all about. Maybe she was just horny. Maybe she was just tired of the guys whose entire effort consisted of a grunt, thinking they were doing her some big favor by daring to offer their cocks not for her pleasure, but their own amusement.

She knew it was a cliché, having a crush on your college professor, but she didn't care. She liked the way his voice lilted, how he made sure to turn around and truly talk to, not just at, the class. She liked how he remembered everyone's names. She liked how he used examples of real companies, straight from the newspaper, to explain things. She liked the way he looked at her, lingering on her for a few seconds longer than everyone else—even if that part was just in her imagination.

She drove the short distance to the school, forgoing coffee and her usual cigarette, wanting to enter as much on her own steam as she could. She didn't want to later be able to blame her "bad behavior" on anyone but herself. She wondered if it was her professor she was so hot for, or this new version of Meredith—Meredith 2.0, as her kids would say—who was shucking off her baggage and tapping into the lusty thoughts she usually kept buried under her pillow.

When she reached Professor Arthur's office, she knocked on the closed door, while looking around the quiet hallway. The school took on a different tone in the early evening, without the rush of students to and fro, their newly freed hormones practically bouncing off the walls. She could pause and look at the actual building, appreciate its history and her place in it. Meredith rounded her shoulders, feeling, for just a moment, like she was heading to the principal's office. Just then the door opened and a tall, slim blonde girl walked out, giving her a shy smile.

Professor Arthur looked up at her and smiled. For a second, her mind went to the two of them; had they been in there enacting the scenarios she'd conjured in her head?

"Meredith, welcome."

"Hi, Professor," she said.

"Ralph, please," he corrected her, and before she could say anything, he added, "I just want you to know I'm glad you're in my class. I think it's wonderful that you're coming back to school. Too many people think that once they've hit a certain age there's no point, or that it's too hard."

She was tempted to ask what age, exactly, that would be, but she didn't. Instead she smiled, trying to beat back the nerves, aware that her outfit was a far cry from her classmate's casual pink T-shirt and jeans. "It's definitely challenging. I'm finding that some of the concepts are over my head. Supply and demand I get…" She trailed off, her throat caught as she watched him watching her, watched his eyes behind his glasses, watched him fidgeting with the pencil in his hand. Who used pencils, anyway?

She waited for him to say something, but he just walked closer to her until he was right in front of her. "You get supply and demand, Meredith?" he asked, looking down at her. She stood, and they were right in front of each other. "Like you're here to supply something to me, like your pussy, and I'm here to demand that you give me more?"

Oh, god. The words were crazy, over-the-top—and they made her instantly, achingly wet. She suddenly didn't care that he was younger, that she was his student, that she wasn't in some preppy uniform or casual chic, but instead, basically naked, save for a dress that did little to hide the nipples pressing against its red fabric, threatening to spill over the purple edges.

"Yes, like that. I want to give you…whatever you want." As

she said it, she realized it was true, because in giving to him, she was gaining so much. She'd been giving and giving and giving ever since she gave birth and now, finally, it was her time to take. Taking orders, taking spankings, taking cock—that's what she wanted.

"I've had my eye on you, Meredith. The way you sit there in class, so attentive when almost everyone else has their heads in their phones or computers. The way you look at me. I want to give you everything you deserve. But first I think you need a spanking. Put your hands on the desk," he said, sounding far older than whatever his actual age was. When he lifted the dress and saw she wasn't wearing panties, he whistled.

"Spread your legs for me, Meredith, so I can look at your pussy." She heard the door's lock click, and then he was kneeling in front of her, breathing on her. "When was the last time someone other than you touched you here?" he asked, running a fingertip along her sex. She shuddered, and he did it again. She pressed back against him but he grabbed one of her asscheeks and pinched it. "Answer me, Meredith. Don't make your teacher angry."

"Two years," she squeaked out, and received a smack on her right cheek, whether as reward or punishment she wasn't sure. She was sure that she was drooling, but there was nothing she could do, not with her head resting on his desk, her arms splayed at her side. She was drooling between her legs, too, especially when he spanked her again. And again.

"When was the last time your ass got spanked, Meredith?"

She was quiet, and now tears rose to her eyes. "Never," she whispered, and felt him again grab her ass, this time with both hands, holding her open. Then he did the same with her pussy lips, gripping them and splaying her wide. She'd wanted to be treated like this, she thought, like a real slut, the kind whose body is up for grabs. "You like that, don't you, Meredith?" he asked, letting go and then giving her a light tap against her pussy lips.

She trembled, then answered in an overloud voice, "Yes."

"That's good. Because I'm going to make you sore today. I'm going to make you so sore that in two days when you sit in my classroom your ass is still going to sting, and I'm going to call on you to make sure you're paying attention, not daydreaming about when I'm next going to take this sweet ass for a ride. Do you understand?"

As he spoke, Ralph had been smacking her all over—her pussy, her upper thigh, her butt. "Yes, I do. I understand."

"Sir," he said. "Call me 'Sir.' We're done with Ralph and Professor. That's not who I am right now. I'm your owner."

He plunged his fingers inside her, and she pressed her fist to her mouth, afraid of what might come out. She wanted him to own her, like this, to take over for her in a way nobody had in she couldn't remember how long. And her body wanted it too; she was so hot between her legs, so tight, so desperate, suddenly, to be filled. He moved, and she kept her eyes closed, not wanting to know what was coming. She found out soon enough. It was a ruler, a metal one, striking hard against both asscheeks. She'd have laughed if the pain hadn't seared its way through her entire body.

"This is what happens when you distract me in class, when you try to make my cock hard." The ruler's edges dug into her skin, stronger and meaner than his hand, but she soon got acclimated to it. She'd never gotten more than a light swat before, but she liked it. She liked being at his mercy, not having to think beyond the initial decision to walk in. The pain was like a door opening to something better, a room to a house she'd never seen before. The blows came down harder and harder and soon the

tears were indeed coming down her cheeks, but they weren't
from the pain. That part she could handle, though she knew
she'd probably have to sit on a cushion. The tears were for all
the other emotions his spanking stirred up.

"How does your ass feel, Meredith?"

"Very good, Sir," she said.

"Louder," he said in a deep voice, grabbing her by the hair
and pressing her tightly to the desk, the threat of what he could
do to her more than enough to make her repeat herself more
forcefully.

"How good?" he asked.

She didn't know how to answer. The heat and pain were
intense, but not too much. Just enough, but...something was
missing. She tingled there, all over. "Good enough that it makes
me want something in my ass."

She wasn't sure where the words had come from. She hadn't
been thinking about that hole, had never really thought about
it, though she knew her peers did, heard their whispers on
Monday mornings, practically saw their asses peeking out over
their tight, low-rise jeans. But now, suddenly, she was, as if he'd
conjured the words out of her mouth, except he hadn't. He'd just
spanked her and now she realized it was true, she wanted his
cock, sight unseen, in her ass.

She felt his thumb pressing against her there and she moaned,
thrashing just enough to get him to press a little deeper. "I see
how much your ass needs to be fucked, Meredith." Every time
he said her name, her cheeks got a little hotter. It was the way
he said it, like he knew everything about her, when he barely
knew a thing. But he did know some things, like how to work
his thumb right there, halfway in, until she clenched around it
tightly. "Hold your cheeks open for me," he said.

She reached behind her to do just that, shocked at how easily she obeyed such a command, and how much she liked it. "That's good," he said. "Now stay like that, because if you don't, I'm going to stop fucking you." Then his fingers were inside her pussy, strong and assured, and she didn't care that it wasn't her ass, as long as he was touching her, getting closer to her, giving her some part of him. "Good girl," he said, and the two words, so basic, so simple, made her melt. She wanted to be a girl, sometimes, not a woman, a schoolgirl whose only assignment was sex, and here she was, taking more fingers—she didn't know how many, but she knew he'd added some.

"Are you ready for my cock, Meredith?" She nodded, though she liked his fingers just fine, actually. "Yes, Sir," she amended, when his fingers stilled inside her.

"You may put your hands down," he said, and she did, resting her head against the desk for a moment, savoring her ass being in the air, being open and wet and wanton like this.

Soon he was back, and she heard him rolling a condom onto his cock. Then he dragged her down from the desk and put her hands on the floor in front of her, so her body made a *V*. Then, without another word, he was inside her. Meredith gasped; either he was huge, or she was so starved for sex that she felt like she might break in two, in a good way. She wanted to touch her clit, but didn't dare, as he drilled into her. This was about her getting fucked, not doing the fucking, and she wanted to keep it that way. She didn't want to work right now, didn't want to supply anything but her body, like this, splayed open wide for her very hot teacher. She felt like a girl in a porn video, and for a second wondered if he had a camera on somewhere taping them. What a horror that would be...but it would also be kind of hot. She smiled as he pulled out, then slammed back in, and she shifted so her *V* was slightly less wide, making his cock stroke her at a different angle.

She kept picturing some innocent student walking in, even though the door was locked, and realized as she started to come that she wouldn't really have minded, at least not this Meredith: slutty Meredith. She wanted someone to know that this was part of who she was too. Ralph knew, and he used that knowledge expertly. She focused on the sensation, familiar but also totally new. She'd never gotten fucked in this position and it felt incredible; when he played with her clit, it felt all the more so. When he slapped her clit, Meredith lost it, trembling and letting herself give over to the climax, tightening around his cock and grunting hard. "That's it," he said, urging her on. "You feel so good around my cock."

She looked back at him and saw him watching them, watching himself going inside her, and that made her do it again, a ripple effect that left her wondering just what exactly he was doing to her. They'd gone far beyond supply and demand now; he was showing, telling, giving, taking—all at once. Then he started fucking her faster, and she braced herself. He didn't need long before he said, "I'm coming," and she felt him cream into the condom, then gently slide out. She stood up and her dress fell down over her waist. She was grateful for it, grateful not to be totally nude after what they'd just done.

"Sit," he said, and once she'd settled herself, he brought her a bottle of water.

"Wow," she said, and laughed, because what else could she do? She wanted to ask if he did this all the time, but there was a knock at the door. He quickly threw the condom in the trash, followed by some tissues, zipped up, wiped his hands with another tissue and then opened the door. She heard him tell the next student to give him a few minutes.

Then there was an awkward silence. She wished momentarily for it to have been a dream. How old was he anyway? "Maybe we could go out on a proper date," he said, lifting her chin to force her to look at him, her face flaming.

"Maybe," she said, suddenly anxious to leave. "But maybe we should wait until the semester ends." Did she mean that? She wasn't sure, but this was so awkward she couldn't tell if what she'd just experienced was worth it.

"So, see you in class on Friday?" he asked.

"See you," she said.

She stood, gathering her things, sure that her escapade was written all over her face. His hand cupped her ass on her way past him, a gentle reminder that she didn't in any way need. She smiled at him, with her mouth, not yet ready to bring her eyes into it. She walked out the door and kept her head high as she heard her shoes clicking on the floor. She thought of stopping at a lingerie store, but realized she wasn't in the mood for something so intimate. Instead, she went to the mall, bought a soda and wandered the stores, sipping loudly, observing her own version of Economics 101. She finished the soda and got lured into a store promising 50 percent off on dresses she didn't need but she walked in anyway, still in a sex stupor. Without buying a bra or panties, she tried on a slinky black dress that was in no way appropriate for school or work. She bought it, and promised herself she'd wear it to class, and then to dinner with Ralph.

Maybe they shouldn't wait until the semester ended, after all.

UNBIDDEN

Brandy Fox

When she hit forty, a raging libido blindsided Brooke. One day she was juggling a family life, giving in to the bloating of age and the exhaustion that hit the minute the kids were in bed. The next, she was sizing up every man between the ages of twenty and sixty, looking them over as meticulously as she did the fruit and vegetables at the market: men in cars waiting at stoplights, grocery store clerks, fellow PTA parents, the carpet cleaner and plumber. Sure, she'd always admired a handsome man. But now it wasn't just looking; it was sweaty, heart-pounding visions of his naked body thrusting away at hers.

Sometimes it didn't even take the sight of a man to turn her on. She could be washing a carrot, hurrying to finish a casserole before meeting the school bus, and her hand would linger along the length of its unusually wide girth. Suddenly she'd be on the kitchen floor, thrusting that carrot into her G-spot. Fantasies whipped through her mind unbidden, sending her to the bedroom at all hours of the day—sometimes when her children were in the next room—overwhelmed with the urge to fondle and fuck herself into oblivion.

"Wow," her doctor friend said, when Brooke confessed the change. "That's your testosterone talking. Now you know how men feel."

"Not men," Brooke corrected. "Boys. Fifteen-year-old boys who haven't yet learned how to tame their hormones. A middle-aged mother is not supposed to be acting that way!" *Especially with carrots,* she thought.

"Consider yourself lucky," her friend said. "Most women who come to my office complain about their lack of libido. Embrace it while you can!"

So Brooke brought her lust into bed with her husband, Calvin. He welcomed it and gave her what she needed when he could. But they had two young children and busy lives that didn't allow him to be her sex slave twenty-four hours a day. She worked off the sexual energy at the gym, where her fat disappeared and her muscles grew. Soon even her minivan and earthy nature couldn't hide that instinctual drive to attract men. For the first time in her life, she began to wear makeup, frequent the hair salon, and buy new, more feminine clothing.

And more and more often, she wondered: What if one of those men actually responded to her longing? Would she—*could she*—hold herself back from someone new, someone, unlike her husband, she hadn't been with for twelve years now? And if not, would it finally satiate her desire?

One Friday, Brooke bought a new dress for a party that night— her friend's fortieth birthday, Brooke noted, chuckling to herself. The material of the sheer black dress clung to her palm-sized breasts, firm tummy and tight ass. The low-cut V-neck exposed more of her chest than she usually allowed. It showed off her best features: long neck, strong shoulders and biceps, the perfect sweep of her collarbone, and a birthmark that beckoned from the top of her cleavage like an invitation to explore the vacant space between her breasts. The material was so thin, her lacy black bra showed through in certain light, and she had to wear a G-string or the lines would look tacky. When the dress was paired with a colorful pendant and flowing shawl, Brooke knew she looked stunning.

After getting ready for the party, she came into the kitchen to wait for the babysitter. When Calvin saw her, he did a double take. His lustful gaze took in every inch of her body. "Whoa," he breathed.

"Is it too much?" Brooke asked innocently, putting her hands on her hips.

He stepped closer and traced the V-neck of her dress. His other hand wandered down her back and onto her rear. "It depends how soon I can get you into bed."

Suddenly, the doorbell rang, and the kids came screaming into the room. Calvin leaned into her ear and whispered, "Later," then gave her a kiss on the cheek and turned away. His quick gesture left her body humming with anticipation.

At the party, Calvin found a group of men talking politics while Brooke settled into a gaggle of fellow first-grade parents. She soon noticed the wandering eyes of men and women alike, flitting down, then up, then down the length of her body as though pulled by a magnet, igniting her insides with the tingly heat of being wanted. She knew it wasn't likely that *everyone* at the party lusted after her, but there was no stopping her naughty mind from lingering on the fantasy.

At one point, she glanced around the room and saw Kyle, a fellow preschool parent from a few years back. She'd always found him very attractive: cropped salt-and-pepper hair, bright blue eyes and prominent cheekbones. It had been at least two years since she'd seen him, and now, unlike before she'd turned forty, her entire body responded with an exquisite ache. She suddenly imagined his mouth leaving a trail of kisses on her neck—instinctually knowing to skip her wildly ticklish collarbone—then across her breasts and down her belly, until finally he reached her navel and...

Brooke squeezed her eyes shut and shook her head free of the image before she made a fool of herself. When she opened them, Kyle was looking right at her.

She smiled and waved meagerly, a bead of sweat forming on the back of her neck. He tilted his head, brow stitched as though trying to figure out who she was. *Great, he probably thinks I'm flirting with him now*, she thought, then brought her attention back to the group.

A minute later, he was by her side. "Brooke?"

She nodded, smiling. "You didn't recognize me."

"Hell, no!" On cue, his gaze wandered up and down her body. "Did you lose weight or something?"

"Just getting to the gym more," she explained.

"Well, it's working. You look great!"

Brooke glanced around the room for Kyle's wife, Jane. "I'm surprised to see you here," Brooke said. "How do you know the birthday girl?"

"I work with her." Kyle locked eyes with Brooke for so long she had to look away, embarrassed.

"So...is Jane here?"

"Yeah, she's somewhere around..." His gaze swept the room. "Not sure where." He glanced at Brooke's nearly empty glass. "Can I get you more wine?"

"Sure," Brooke replied, thinking she could use another drink with all this attention.

He was back soon with two drinks, one for her and one for him. They wedged their way back into the group and chatted and drank for another hour. Every so often, Brooke would catch Kyle's gaze. He would tilt his head and smile, or furrow his brow at her as though trying to figure something out. He always managed to bring the conversation back to her, and when her glass was empty again, he refilled it.

Once, Brooke saw Calvin across the room, cornered by one of their more annoying friends. *I should go rescue him*, Brooke thought. Then she caught Kyle's eye, their glances now turning into long, lingering looks full of innuendo, and decided against it.

She didn't realize just how tipsy she was until she was laughing so hard at a joke that she had to grasp Kyle's shoulder to stay upright and she almost peed in her pants. "I'm going to the bathroom," she announced, then veered away, surreptitiously holding the wall as she went down the hallway. When she found the bathroom already occupied, she wandered up the stairs and to another one, vaguely aware that her body was acting more quickly than she was thinking.

Peeing was almost an orgasm in itself. Her body was already on fire from all those sweeping glances and thoughts of Kyle's bare chest. She spread her legs wider and fingered her wet nub, hoping for a quick release.

Someone cleared his throat outside the bathroom. She froze, listened again and heard more sounds of a person waiting. Reluctantly, she stopped touching herself and finished up in the bathroom.

When she opened the door, Kyle was in the hallway. He moved toward her so suddenly it caused Brooke to step back quickly, knocking her off-kilter. Kyle caught her, held her shoulders and gently led her backward into the bathroom.

He closed the door behind them and stepped so close she

could taste the wine on his breath. He reached up and fondled her pendant. "This is gorgeous. Is it Murano glass?"

Brooke's breath came in short gasps. She felt her nipples harden just knowing how close his hands were to them. "Yes. How did you know?"

"I've been to Venice," he replied, rubbing his thumb across its smooth surface.

"With Jane?" It came out before she could think, but she knew why. She wanted to snap him out of this weird little moment so she wouldn't have to say no. Because she wasn't sure she could.

He let the pendant drop. "Yes, with Jane."

Brooke thought she'd succeeded in making him back off. But instead, he took a step closer and pressed his leg between her thighs.

Brooke swallowed, trying hard to keep her mind on her husband rather than on the intense burning between her legs. *Calvin, Calvin, Calvin,* she thought to herself. *The man I've loved for twelve years. My lover, my best friend. Calvin.* She closed her eyes to get a picture of him in her mind: that pale, angelic face; those deep forest green eyes that had drawn her in the moment they met.

The knee between her thighs pressed harder, brushing against her groin, sending a wave of electricity from her belly to her throat. Despite all her efforts to resist, she leaned her head back and moaned. *This is it,* Brooke thought. *This is the fantasy I've had for the past year—some hot guy finding me so irresistible he can't keep his hands off me.*

Then Brooke felt something soft flutter against her collarbone, tickling her so intensely her hand flew up to scratch it. Instead of reaching her chest, she clocked the side of Kyle's head. "Oh, sorry!" Brooke giggled.

A look of irritation swept over Kyle's face, then disappeared. He leaned in to kiss her chest again, but Brooke's hands were on his shoulders before he could make the same mistake twice.

"Wait," she muttered, halfheartedly pushing him away. All that strength training and for what? She was melting right into a near-stranger's arms, nothing more than a sleazy, cheating bastard who didn't even know about her ticklish spot. Maybe that's all she was, too—a slut who'd do anything to get off. Would Calvin forgive her if she blamed it on the alcohol? On a thoughtless moment, her out-of-control hormones? A very convincing voice in her head told her to go for it, she deserved this: her dream come true after all these months of testosterone overload driving her to near insanity. *You're forty. You might never get this chance again. Live a little!*

Kyle leaned in to her ear and whispered, "Brooke. You are so hot."

She remembered Calvin's promise of "later" before the party, the look of genuine lust he still had for her. She knew he would never corner some random drunk woman, no matter how hot she looked. Calvin would never, ever cheat on Brooke. And yet, she knew in her heart that he would forgive her for cheating on him.

But Kyle wasn't the one she wanted.

"Wait," she said again, more confident this time. Her hands moved from his shoulders to his chest, and she pushed him firmly away.

He stepped back, pulling his knee away. Instantly, her lucidity returned.

"Kyle. We're married. This doesn't feel right."

"It doesn't?" he asked, coming toward her again.

She put up her hand. "No...well, yes. It feels...but no, I don't want to do it."

He put his hands in his pockets and took a step back, looking defeated. "That's too bad. It would have been fun." A smile snuck across his face, despite his clear attempt to look hurt. "If you ever change your mind, let me know, okay?" And then he left.

Brooke leaned against the wall for another minute, taking deep breaths, trying to slow her racing heart. She cupped her hands under the faucet and took a long drink of water. She patted her face and chest with a towel, took another deep breath, then left the bathroom to find Calvin and take him home.

The moment Brooke saw the babysitter's taillights leave their driveway, she dragged Calvin to the couch—she didn't think she could make it all the way to their bedroom. She removed her underwear in a slow striptease, watching his eyes grow wide with delight. When she began to slink out of her dress, Calvin said, "No, wait," and pulled her on top of him. "I like this dress." He traced the V-neck then dipped his fingers underneath it, inside her bra, teasing her nipple. She squealed with delight, relieved at how *right* it felt to be with Calvin and not Kyle.

Calvin caressed her body with his gaze, then settled on her eyes. "You are so hot," he said.

"You're not the first guy to say that to me tonight," Brooke said easily. It even felt right to tell him the truth.

"Oh, really?" Calvin's finger continued to circle her nipple, threatening to make her forget about honesty and just get on with the fun. "Who else?"

"Someone at the party. Kyle from the preschool. Remember him?"

Calvin shook his head. Brooke assumed he'd never actually met Kyle.

"Anyway...he made a pass at me."

"What did he do?"

"He cornered me in the bathroom and stuck his knee in my groin."

Calvin's finger stopped circling. He moved his hand down her body, across her buttock, then brushed her labia with a finger. "You mean here?" he asked, his eyes twinkling.

She shuddered, the pressure in her belly unbearable. Within seconds, the bulge in his jeans grew hard. She pressed into it, her hungry pussy wanting to eat it up along with his fingers.

He pulled them away, back to her ass. "And then what happened?"

She sighed, desperate for his fingers to be back on her swollen clit. But she knew he deserved to hear more. She took a deep breath and tried to remember. "Well...he persisted for a while, and I was pretty drunk...I know that's not an excuse, it just made it harder to stop him."

"Stop him from doing what?" Calvin asked. His eyes sparkled with curiosity.

"From touching my chest, and..."

Calvin's fingers slid between her legs, one of them dipping gently inside her, then spreading her warm juices around and around.

Brooke paused, her breathing ragged, uneven. "And kissing my collarbone, which you know I can't stand."

Calvin's finger slid back inside her, then another, and another. Brooke pressed down into them, rocking back and forth, arching her body. Then, abruptly, he removed them.

"So what did you do?"

Brooke shuddered, moaning loudly. "Calvin...I need you now..."

He just stared at her, waiting.

"When I came to my senses, I told him to back off, that we're both married and I didn't want to cheat on you." As she talked,

Brooke ground her hips into Calvin's rock-solid bulge, then lifted her pelvis toward his warm mouth, that supple tongue she knew would make her come instantly.

Calvin just watched her, smiling wickedly. He slid his hands all the way up her sides to cup her breasts and pinch her taut nipples.

"Is that what you want? To have sex with another man?"

Brooke locked eyes with Calvin. He knew her better than any other man, sexually and in every other way. They'd made love thousands of times, and there was no way a fling with someone else would ever compare.

"No," Brooke said with absolute certainty. "I just want you. And your tongue on my cunt. Right now." She grabbed his shoulders and pushed his head between her open legs. He slid down the couch, his tongue welcoming her drenched sex, matching its desire, dipping and twirling, bathing it in his steamy breath as she rode his face. Within seconds, waves of pleasure jerked her body so hard she had to hold on to the wall to keep from falling over. She screamed, forgetting about the kids upstairs, the neighbors next door, the world outside Calvin's mouth between her legs.

He had his pants off before she'd even recovered. He slid back up the couch and pulled her hips toward his eager cock standing at attention. It slid in quickly, making a beeline for her sweet spot like an old companion. Brooke sighed at the ease of their passion. She rocked while he thrust, their movements so familiar, so perfectly timed after years of practice. She spread her hands over his broad chest and braced herself as she exploded with the pleasure of knowing this man wasn't just a fantasy. He was all hers, every last inch.

SOMETHING
TO RUIN

Amelia Thornton

I could feel the soft scratchiness of the grass tickling my cheek as my face pressed closer to the ground, my eyes adjusting to focus on the depth of green and the pair of tiny ladybugs delicately crawling along in front of me. I had never quite noticed before just how vividly red they could be, like little droplets of blood against towers of emerald, and I wondered why it took having my face crushed into the earth to really appreciate nature like this.

I couldn't see him, but I knew he was still there, calmly positioned on the comforting softness of the picnic blanket, surveying the sight of my bottom presented to him, my knees tucked neatly beneath my torso, arms stretched out in front of me. I had done as he'd asked and worn "something to ruin," meaning a plain white sundress with a cornflower-blue print I'd picked up from the secondhand shop. "Something to ruin" always meant trouble.

"Come here, Susie."

Gingerly, I picked myself up from the ground, dusting off my hands and smoothing out the fabric of my dress, smiling up at him as I did so. He smiled back at me, motioning for me to join him, watching me eagerly bounce over to the blanket and curl up next to him, planting a kiss on his cheek as I did so. The sun was already warm on my pale skin, and all around us stretched fields of faded green, dotted with clusters of yellow wildflowers and the smell of summer, under a never-ending canopy of blue sky and hazy heat. We had bought an old wicker hamper especially for the occasion of a picnic, but in typical English fashion had been faced with nothing but rain and clouds for all of the months of June and July, and now at last had the opportunity to make use of it. Carefully, I unpacked the plates and glasses, laid out potato salad and pork pies and all of the other things that never tasted quite right unless eaten outdoors, then served him a plate of all his favorite things.

I knew he was watching me, though, looking at me in the way that makes me feel both slightly anxious and overwhelmingly loved at the same time. I knew he was planning something. Sure enough, just as I was about to take a big bite of cold chicken, he laid his hand gently on my arm and shook his head.

"Put your hands behind your back."

Hesitatingly, I obeyed him, placing the chicken back on my plate, folding my arms neatly in place, wondering what he would be thinking of, what he would want from me now. He knows how difficult I find it to do as I am told, much as I adore the feelings that come with it. Whether not speaking unless spoken to or keeping still until he moves me, it always seems so much more frustratingly difficult to do something myself that could much better be aided by wrist cuffs, blindfolds and gags. But at the same time, that is why being with him excites me so much: the sheer, simplistic beauty of submitting to him without all of those things, without anything that makes my job any easier, without having any excuse to not give myself and my obedience completely and purely. He knows that.

Tenderly, he broke off a piece of chicken and held it to my lips, his fingers brushing against my cheek as he offered it to me, his eyes looking straight into mine. I took it in my teeth, chewing it slowly, noticing how different it tasted now that I could not feed it to myself. Like I was a pet. Piece by piece he fed me each thing from my plate, but always with his hand, letting me lick the remnants from his fingers like a hungry little kitten, pausing in between to eat his own food in a perfectly civil manner. The dessert I had packed was a little Tupperware box of strawberries sprinkled with sugar, which he opened and scooped a handful of them out, the juice dribbling across his palm, sweet and sticky. My eyes met his, wondering if I was allowed to move yet, but he simply rested his hand on the ground, against the wool of the blanket, watching for my reaction. Patiently, carefully, I repositioned myself onto my knees, never moving my arms from behind me, imagining them bound in invisible chains, then lowered my face to his hand. I could smell the sweetness of the sugar so close to my nostrils, breathing in the scent of the fields around us combined with the sharpness of the fruit, and I took a piece in my mouth.

The juice slipped down my throat, sweet and fragrant, each bite more delicious than the last. As I swallowed each piece, my tongue ran across the rough surface of his palm, lapping at the last of it, wishing his hand would clamp across my mouth and hold me down the way he knows I love, hold me breathless and captive as he took me in every way he desired. Gently, my lips closed around his fingertips, sucking each one, taking them deep inside my mouth, planting tiny kisses across his knuckles and tender bites on the heel, adoringly worshipping the hands that control me so effortlessly. I love his hands, the way they touch me and possess me and pleasure me. I wanted his hands inside me right then and there, and hoped beyond hope he would want that, too.

"I think it's time to go for a walk."

He lifted my head and smiled at my frustration, motioning my arms to return to my sides and for me to stand. I try so hard not to act like a petulant little brat at times like these, but it's so difficult when I know what I want, and he knows what I want, and he still won't give it to me. Ignoring my sulky pout, he picked up the battered leather gym bag he had insisted on carrying with us all the way from the car to the picnic spot, took hold of my hand and led me purposefully off toward the woods, leaving all of our picnic things where they were.

"What about the hamper?" I whined, struggling to keep up with his determined pace. "Somebody might steal it! Really, we should just stay where we are. Don't you want to finish your food?"

He just smiled at me, recognizing my usual reluctance to enter into any of his schemes, as most likely it would result in some part of my anatomy becoming very sore, but chose to ignore it.

"You do worry about the silliest things, Susie. Surely you should be more concerned about me taking you into the woods all alone than whether somebody will steal our picnic hamper?"

"Well, yes, of course I am, that wasn't what I said, I just said that we—"

"I know what you're saying," he interrupted me calmly, looking at me in that way that I always find so deliciously disconcerting. "I know what you're saying, and I know you want to come with me anyway. Don't you?"

I just frowned, knowing full well he was right, and squeezed his hand a little tighter as we reached the edge of the woods. Stumbling, I followed him through the trees, my steps crisscrossing over fallen branches and leaf-strewn ditches. The sunlight fell in dappled shadows across the uneven ground, highlighting patches of dark green ferns and towering silver birches, scattered petals of fuchsia foxgloves and carpets of thick, emerald moss growing over fallen tree trunks. I knew wherever he was leading me would be somewhere I wanted to go; it was just a question of what I would go through to get there.

Finally, we reached a spot he found suitable: a broad, strong tree trunk surrounded by patches of moss and shrubbery, gaps in the branches above allowing strips of sunlight to fall across it, utterly silent except for the rustle of breeze in the leaves. Pausing, he took my hand and delicately positioned me with my back against the tree, his eyes scanning for the symmetry of my body centered against it, the tiny details that made me love him all the more. Kissing each of my eyelids in turn, he whispered for me to close them, before leaving me in self-imposed darkness. Taking a deep breath, I relaxed my body back against the tree, feeling the curve of my spine bend into it, and readied myself for whatever he might wish.

What he wished, however, was not what I expected. I felt the soft scratch of hemp ropes dragging across my bare skin, the sound of him looping them around the trunk of the tree, and a shiver of excitement flickered through me. He had always told me he wouldn't tie me up until he knew I would submit without it, much as I pleaded with him. He said there was no use in forcing me to do something when what he really wanted was to see me willingly surrender myself, which, although challenging, had made each surrender all the more sweet. I felt a glimmer of pride as I realized he accepted I was his now, and knew how much I craved the feeling of restriction, with the rope biting into my skin, making me struggle and wriggle and sigh with contentment. He knew what I needed.

I gasped as he pulled the ropes tighter, feeling them cutting into my flesh and binding me even closer to the rough bark of the tree. I could feel it under my fingertips, coarse and uneven, but even more uncomfortable as it dug into my back and the soft skin of my arms. Despite my longing, there was still part of me that wanted to protest, to tell him to cut me loose, to run wildly through the forest back to the safety of our picnic blanket, but to me that is the beauty of rope: to desire escape but to willingly be imprisoned, to feel the pressure of something that prevents my movement, yet to know there is no place that I feel safer than when trapped like this.

He smiled at me as he recognized those thoughts, and kissed me gently on the forehead before circling another length of rope across the tops of my breasts and looped into the one below them, cutting into my chest and forcing my upper back tighter against the tree, immobilizing my torso entirely.

I struggled against my restraints, whimpering at the sensation, the realization of my own helplessness tingling in my stomach. He was so close to me now, his breath hot on my neck, his mouth just inches from mine, his hands running across the thin cotton of my dress and sending shivers through me as his fingertips brushed lightly against my hardened nipples. I wanted to open my eyes so much, to see the trees around me, to look into his face and see the desire in it. But I couldn't.

"What do you want, my Susie?" he murmured in my ear, his hands perilously close to the tops of my thighs, the fabric of my dress now seeming an oppressive weight on my skin, preventing his touch.

"You," I whispered back, praying for his fingers to just reach for the hem of the dress, to slip beneath, to dance across the aching expanse of my skin and beyond, to reach inside and feel the wet heat of me surrounding him. Just one touch from him was always enough to make me gasp, to make the breath catch in my lungs, to make me want more and more and more...but he wouldn't even give me that. Every inch of me felt like it was sparking with electricity, alive with sensation, longing for him, inwardly pleading for him to just abandon his restraint and give in to his own need, instead of torturing me with mine.

The flat of his palm was against my thigh now, smoothing the cotton down, stroking it gently, enjoying the knowledge that he had me just where he wanted me.

"Please?"

He just laughed, a long, low laugh in the back of his throat; then, before I could even catch my breath, he'd taken hold of the edge of the cotton and ripped it ferociously, the material tearing in a jagged line across my legs, hanging in tatters where it had once lain flat. In its absence I could feel what an agonizing barrier that thin layer of cotton had been, the sensation of his thumb tracing lines along my bare thigh now even more electrifying. A breeze rustled the leaves of the trees, caressing me with coolness, the rough bark still digging into me, all of nature surrounding me, my whole body alive with feeling, yet deprived of such simple senses.

Softly, he kissed my cheek, and then his touch was gone. I knew he was near, from the sounds of his footsteps against twigs and leaves, circling me like an animal lusting after its prey. I knew he was there, yet I couldn't stop wondering what he was doing, analyzing each sound, willing my eyes to stay shut despite the burning need to look at him, to see what he was planning to do to me.

Minutes later, I found out. A slow, prickling burn was

building against my right forearm, more like an itch at first, climbing to a furious, fiery sting. Biting my lip, I held back my squeals, wriggling against my bonds as the nettles crept up my arm and across my breastbone, down my left arm, across the shredded remains of my dress and down to my thighs. I squeezed my eyes shut with all my might, my mind filled with the image of him before me, a soft smile upon his lips as he watched me squirm, savoring the thought of his pleasure from my discomfort. I knew he wouldn't be foolish enough to hold the stem of the nettles himself, and couldn't help but admire his sense of forward planning to have thought to bring a rag, or a handkerchief, or whatever else he would be using to stop the leaves from burning him while they raced like needles across my flesh.

"Open your eyes."

Brightness flooded my vision, sunlight and birds and leaves and trees, as he pulled his bare hand away, just for one moment, then brought it down against my leg with stinging ferocity. That one smack felt like it reverberated through my whole body, taking me away from my eyes and back into my skin, sensation shooting from that one, burning spot on my inner thigh right up my spinal cord and out to every single nerve ending in my being. Before I could think about anything else, a smack on my opposite thigh landed, even harder than the first, followed by two farther down. The nettle burns now a dull, forgotten agony, my eyes met his, pleading with him not to stop, my lids fluttering as he struck me again and again, each hit like a pulse of feeling through my limbs. Over and over he rained his blows against my legs, a rhythmic symphony of intensity dancing across the surface of my flesh. It was so strange how he could have done exactly the same thing without tying me, and I would have remained motionless just as he told me, but it just would never have felt the same.

I yelped as his smacks finally stopped and his hands roughly groped the burning marks they had made, squeezing my soft soreness, his whole body pressed into mine, his mouth on my neck and shoulders, fierce kisses across my collarbone. It felt like my whole body was plugged into an outlet, zinging with electricity as his kisses grew ever more insistent, aching with need to have him touch me where I needed it most of all, where I felt I would explode if he didn't push his fingers inside and...

Dropping to his knees in the dirt and leaves, his teeth sank into the stinging red marks his hands had made, sucking and biting and kissing and licking. I could feel the throbbing insistence in my clit growing stronger and stronger as his mouth covered my thighs with feeling, the need to have him take me now almost unbearable. *Please, please, please, please...* A strangled cry escaped my throat as his tongue reached my wetness, running long, slow strokes across the curve of my cunt, each ending in a tiny flick on my swollen clit. Every movement made my whole body jerk in my bonds; that one, teasing dart of his tongue making me yearn for more, until at last his lips closed around my clit, surrounding me with warmth.

"Please," I managed to gasp, "please..."

His fingers thrust inside me in response, curling toward his mouth as his tongue circled my clit, rhythmically tapping against my G-spot as sparks of pleasure flew through me. It was so strange to hear the birds cheerfully chirping around me as I writhed against tightly bound rope, my legs struggling to wrap around him and bring him even closer to me; to see the branches of the trees swaying above my head as I clenched myself tighter and tighter around his pounding fingers. I could feel myself getting closer and closer, like I was climbing a mountain and nearing the peak, standing on the edge of the cliff and waiting to fall off. So he pushed me off.

It felt like it was happening in slow motion as ecstasy ripped through each atom of my being, starting with my clit and radiating outward in pulses of hot, glowing energy. I could feel myself making sound but I couldn't quite recognize it, like I was outside of my body watching it react in ethereal release, not even able to control my vocal chords anymore. Tiny aftershocks emanated all the way to my fingertips as he got to his feet and stood in front of me, his piercing blue eyes looking into mine, his hand pressed hard and flat against my cunt, grounding me, bringing me back to him. I wanted him now more than ever.

"My Susie," he murmured, his tongue tracing the edge of my ear, lazily flicking the soft flesh of my lobe. "I'm going to untie you now, and then I'm going to fuck you on the ground, in the dirt, in the mud. You're going to stay still until I tell you otherwise. Do you understand?"

I nodded obediently, mutely, my mind and my words still floating somewhere above me as he loosened the ropes. My whole body was still pounding as he coiled them up neatly and placed them back in his bag, anticipation tight inside me, clouds of orgasm still drifting through my limbs yet tensing in the knowledge of what was to come. It was always a wonder to me how he managed to stay so calm all the time, so controlled. I was always the one breathlessly pleading, abandoned to my desire, while he remained ever the gentleman, watching me with calculated interest. It made me want to shatter that veneer, bring him to my level of want, watch him lose everything inside me as he took what he needed. But which of us was really taking, I could never quite tell.

With him standing in front of me, I could see the outline of his cock straining against his smart gray trousers, his hand gently rubbing against it, teasing me with my own motionlessness. I wanted to feel it inside my mouth, beneath my hands; but instead I stood there, physically free but still in bondage.

"Get on your knees."

Delicately, I lowered myself to the ground, amongst the prickly twigs and crunching dead leaves. I love the way he commands me, the way he tells me exactly what he wants but never harshly, his voice always calm and even and polite, even when telling me to do things that are far from polite in themselves. I love the way I know that I never need to guess at what he wants, as he will just tell me to do it. I find such beautiful simplicity in the way he loves me.

Stroking my hair, he took out his cock and offered it to my waiting mouth, with just one tiny, almost inaudible, intake of his breath as I closed my mouth around it. There is something about sucking his cock that relaxes me, makes me feel calm and centered and like nothing in the world matters anymore, like I could stay there on my knees forever and never want for anything more. With long, deep strokes I took him deeper and deeper, my lips tight around him, my tongue pressing hard against the underside as he gradually rocked himself rhythmically inside me, feeling his thickness filling my mouth. I looked up at him, seeing trees and sky around him, feeling his fingers twisted in my hair, his eyes half closed in pleasure, and fell in love with him all over again.

Just as I was beginning to close my eyes and really lose myself in the sensation of it, he pulled away from me, making me whimper at the shock of it, which of course made him smile. Gently, he laid me against the ground, my back finding sharp sticks and rough branches scratching between my shoulder blades, but I didn't care. All I cared about was how his strong hands were reaching out to part my legs, his cock against my cunt so close I could almost swallow it with my pussy if I tried hard enough, his eyes looking straight into mine as he finally sank himself within me, making me shudder and gasp and rock my hips in fluid motion to bring him closer to me. The way he fucks me is not like any other man has fucked me, hard and soft at the same time, violent and loving, brutal and gentle. Pulling my knees farther up, I twisted my legs around his back, drawing him deeper within me, pleading inwardly for him to fuck me harder, harder, harder...

His thrusts became more forceful, intensity building inside me as every inch of me became reignited, each stroke seeming to fill me so exactly, it was as if we were made for each other. I reached out for him, pulling his mouth toward mine, forcing my tongue inside him with such hunger and need and desperate abandon, feeling his own desire responding, my beloved, my other half. I know his body so well now, I can feel it when he's nearing his peak, when his muscles tense and his breathing becomes shallow, and all of my energy is focused on feeling him and hearing his breath, those sensations almost mirrored in my own body. That moment, when he finally releases, when all of his control is abandoned, is always so blissful to me; his spasms and cries and animal roars, like those of a beast savaging me, filling me with such contentment it is almost like coming again myself.

His satiated body collapsed onto mine, his arms surrounding me and protecting me and holding me close. I could feel his heart hammering in his chest as it pressed against my own, his heart and my heart together, like drumming in the near-silent forest. Above us, the birds were still singing sweetly, the breeze still shivering through the trees. I can think of nothing more natural than my love for him.

GUITAR HERO

Kin Fallon

He picked up his guitar and strummed it, idly at first, casually. She watched his thick, heavy hands moving across the board in wide strokes. It was hypnotic, restful, and she began to relax. He changed to a beautiful melody, picking each note with a finger or thumb. Anoushka watched his fingers, marveling at how fast they could work, at how delicate and precise the tips of thick fingers of rough hands could be. She felt herself sinking in the rhythm and wondered how her boyfriend didn't get lost himself, how he could think fast enough to move from string to string so seamlessly, so accurately.

Looking to Mark's face, she saw his half-open gray-green eyes, as distant as the stars, as close as her pulse. *Lost in his own way,* she thought. It wasn't concentration keeping him in tune but a flow, a deep sensual memory that called the right fingertip to the right string at the right time. He was truly in tune with his guitar, one with it inside the strings' music, their vibrations, their changes and movements, rises and falls.

Mark was most beautiful when he was like this. He pick\
up the speed to a desperate rhythm, fingers flickering back and
forth, seeming sometimes to bring out two separate sounds that
quickly dissolved into a single one, rising and falling again. The
tempo increased another step change and furiously reached a
peak of high-pitched, longer-waving wails.

He stopped, so alive, so awake, so turned on. He lifted the
guitar gently from his lap and, leaning over, placed it carefully
back on its stand. His body seemed changed, as if the music had
awakened him and brought him a new life. He sat back on the
edge of his seat, pushing his ass back onto it, then moving his
hips forward, repositioning himself from his crotch outward, a
pulse of energy running down his thighs and calves, up through
his hidden stomach, chest and broad shoulders and down
through his very visible muscular arms past the thick leather
strap he wore on his wrist, to his skillful hands.

Anoushka looked up to his face, his life-giving lips, his long
hair—straight but wild, brown but with a hint of dirty blond.
His face seemed eager, hungry. He let his eyes, green now, strong,
fall on her, into her. In that moment she knew that he was going
to fuck the shit out of her and he wasn't going to wait.

"Unbutton your shirt." She moved her hands to the bottom
button. "Start at the top," he corrected and she started to undo
herself until she was a button below the bottom of her bra.
"Stop." She stopped, just a little exposed, the flesh of her small
curves visible. "Pull the sides so I can see more." She complied.
She could see he was starting to enjoy himself, she could see
him coming alive to her, focusing his attention on her. "More
than that, stretch the fabric…more than that…pull the shirt
under your tits." She pulled the shirt, her breasts pushed up and
together even as they strained outward against the constricting
material. She ventured a question, "Like this?"

"Like that," came the reply. "Now pull down your bra." She pulled the bra down. It was tighter and pushed her breasts up into a more obvious, more obscene out-spilling of flesh. She felt her chest swell as if it had become the center of her and saw him staring at her framed beauty, focused, awestruck; she saw his own straining. He touched himself through his jeans without realizing it, his mind, his body all directed toward her. Her nipples hardened in response to his gaze.

He grabbed her waist, picked her up and turned her so that she knelt on the couch, her legs on the seat, her feet dangling over the edge, her body leaning forward against the cushioned back, her backside sticking out.

"Pull up your skirt." She pulled up her skirt, exposing her thighs and private parts and expansive ass covered in red cotton. "Pull your knickers between your asscheeks." She pulled so the knickers became a tight red strip of cotton revealing the two large mounds of her rear on either side. Mark grabbed her ass roughly then licked and slapped as he moved his face down lower between her legs. His eyes followed the pulled red cotton riding through the line of her ass to the stopping point, a thin strip of red stained darker with wetness and want and then the bulge of her hidden fleshy lips squashed between the cotton.

"Open your legs." She parted herself more, feeling her wetness opening farther. She heard him swallow before continuing. "Pull the material between your pussy lips." She did it so that just that thin strip covered her entrance and her engorged lips spilled over either side. "Wiggle it," he instructed, and she whimpered as the material dragged against her clit between the separated flesh. "Hold it to one side." The wet center of her hole was exposed as she moved the red material, and she felt Mark's hot breath on her. She felt him pull the cotton away from her and heard the rip as he disposed of the barrier with his hands.

Then his face was where she wanted it, sucking between her legs, wet on her wetness. He pulled away to look at her and slipped two fingers into her hole, watching them disappearing in and out of her as she started to moan. She pulled her hips up a little and instinctively he pushed down on the two fingers, nudging against the front wall inside of her, giving and taking away the pressure to a slow beat. His thumb took a little of the wetness from her entrance and then curved around and up to find her fattened clit. He massaged it from side to side before joining the rhythm of the fingers inside her. He squeezed and released, inside and out, as if holding all of her pleasure in the palm of his hand. She moaned louder as he played her skill-fully, her heat rising, her sensations flowing through his hand, through her deepest parts. Her body was awakened and alive; she wanted all of him. "Fuck me, Mark," she spoke with a gasp to punctuate her urgency. "Mark, fuck me."

He pulled out his hand, leaving the gap inside her, the open hole: wet, ready, wanting him. She felt his body against her, she felt him at her entrance, in her wetness. She felt him slip inside. She felt his hardness touching her sensitized walls, felt his heat on her awakened flesh; she felt the expanse of him filling her and then his movement, his perfect movement. He thrust along and through her, filling her with desire and its satisfaction, wanting and giving.

As he thrust inside, he leaned to cover her with his body, his mouth on her neck sucking, biting. His hands were on her breasts, the rough palms cupping and grabbing, rubbing. The delicate dexterous tips of his fingers squeezing and turning her nipples. She felt his breath and his life as he licked near her ear, and she enjoyed all of his weight on her.

Each time he sank inside of her, she felt herself holding him there in her center, the hot closeness of him deep inside, the slight easing of the weight on her back as all the muscles of his body pulled hard and tight, his hips pressing forward against her as she strained back against him, each wanting to be deeper, closer.

She felt his body weight against her again as he relaxed slightly and they rode the wave toward the next thrust, in and out, as the pressure and movement from his crotch, rising and falling, seemed to expand outward through her, taking control of their whole bodies.

Her breasts, still framed by her bra, felt the last of his touch as he pulled his hands away, leaving the hot imprint of his skillful caress over the tingling flesh and her nipples vibrating with the memory of his masterful finger work. He moved his hands down to rest his palms on her sides, his fingers curved around her hips as all attention fell to their shared center, his movements hungrier, faster; the pulse inside her louder, crying out for its release. Her breasts shuddered as he banged hard against her, his breath now in tune with her moans. She drove back hard against him as he thrust into her vigorously.

She felt her heat rise to its final peak as he tensed and plowed into her with a final extra force, and she held him there a second longer, feeling her heat pour into him as he poured himself into her. Twice more for joy he slowly rolled into her, filling her. He held her, their bodies together at last as she forgot everything but their feeling deep inside her, their life and pleasure, their stillness and movement, their silence and music.

ODE TO A MASTURBATOR

Aimee Herman

I am leaving in three weeks and I don't even know your name. I am going to miss the sounds I have created in my mind for the music your palm makes when it mashes against your erect dick. You are tall, even when tilted against your wall, which I believe is painted white or some pale color. Your hair is dark like soil and long, always pulled back in a ponytail. If I had courage or confidence, I might talk to you. I know where you live, where you work, what you drive.

I am thirty-one years old and currently work as a server at an all-you-can eat Brazilian steakhouse. Most of my shift is spent watching various-sized humans devouring as much protein as they can, in the form of meat brought to them on skewers, which is then sliced thinly and placed into salivating mouths, chewed enough times to get through the gristle and blood and then swallowed. The competing scents of meat from various animals and limbs has caused me to become vegetarian. It is just too much to take sometimes. However, the pay is good and I met my boyfriend here. We don't have to mention him, though; it doesn't seem fair to either of us.

I know you have a wife. She is blonde with enough curves to appear like a cursive lowercase *q*. Her tits are swollen like flesh-covered marshmallows swelling out of her tops. My tits are small and unclaimed by bras or cleavage. But maybe you need change. I have less to hold and play with, but my nipples are hard like thimbles. They are expressive and overdramatic. One boyfriend even called them challenging. I don't know your wife's name or what she does for a living, but I know that she holds your ears when you eat away at her cunt and scratches at your head when she is just about to come.

I like to pretend that you know I am watching you, from below your window, as I walk my dog and pause just as we approach your apartment building. I first noticed you on a Thursday evening at close to six. I looked up for some reason. Your giant window, which exposed your living room, was also exposing you. I didn't see your face then, though I noticed your hand moving up and down with such speed that I worried about possible skin erosion. I was shocked and turned on, frozen at the image of you fucking yourself.

At the restaurant where I work, I am not naïve about what happens below the tables. Meat can be a turn-on to carnivorous men who are paying twenty-five dollars for unlimited flesh. I have seen men in ties and wingtips fondling their wives/girlfriends/mistresses' thighs with their sausage-like fingers, squeezing their way toward panty lines and neatly manicured bushes. There are some nights I yearn for you to walk in and request a table. As I lead you to your seat, you press your erection into me. My thighs part and with each bite of picanha, alcantra or linguica you take, your eyes grow even needier for me. You leave your blonde wife, who nibbles on prosciutto or hearts of palm from the salad bar, and retreat outside for a breath of fresh air. I'm outside pretending to smoke a cigarette, which I no longer care to smoke, but use as an excuse to leave my station.

"I see you watching me," you say.

"I didn't...I wasn't sure if you noticed."

"I work harder when I know you are watching."

Then I am bold enough to take your hand, which smells like garlic marinade and your wife's perfume probably made by a pop star or aging diva, and place it under my skirt that ends just above my knees. I'm not wearing underwear in this fantasy because women never do in imaginings such as these. You fondle my bush and appreciate the way I've grown it longer than your wife's and then slide into my cunt, claiming it as yours. As you turn one finger into two and then three, I remind myself that I am at work and your wife with inflated lips and bleached teeth is waiting for you in the restaurant. I cannot come. Even in my fantasy.

It is a Sunday and I know you have today off from the hardware store where you work, just six blocks away. My house is full of boxes and blank walls and I cannot bear to think of leaving you. My neck hurts from standing outside your window; where are you today? What dirty thoughts throw you against the wall with hand over dick and come shooting upward? I need you.

As I am about to continue on with my dog, I notice you walking from your kitchen into your living room. You are so long and tall. No clothing claims your skin and I love how hair haunts only small patches of your body: around your nipples, a tightrope toward your belly button and a dash over your stomach. You are standing almost as erect as your dick, which is more narrow than thick, but long enough to impress. I know where this is going.

"What are you looking at?"

Blonde woman with gym-membership abs and false eyelashes interrupts my lustful voyeurism and I immediately recognize her. Shit. Your wife.

"Umm, I thought I saw a bird carrying a worm." What?

"Are you staring into my window? I live there. With my husband. Who are you?"

I never had any interest in exchanging words with your wife, whose nose looks more expensive than my student loan debt. But I couldn't just stand there, silent.

"I'm Kelly," I gracefully extend my hand for her to shake, which she does, piercing my palm with her press-on lacquered nails.

"Do you know my husband? You look familiar to me."

"I work at..." Why does it matter? "I live in the house at the end of this street. I don't know your husband but I'm a huge fan of his dick." Wouldn't it be great if I really said that? "I live in the house at the end of this street. I don't know your husband, but I happened to notice that he's...preoccupied."

She looks up with her bright blue eyes enhanced by contact lenses and good lighting and sees him: her husband, the masturbator.

"You're disgusting. Stop staring at him."

And because I know my time is almost up in this city, I look at her and smile, exposing my off-white, crooked teeth. "He has a really impressive cock."

Even after the words come out, I can't believe I have spoken them. Your wife, whose neck reveals her true age, is quite shocked, too.

"You are filthy," she says, walking away and shaking her surgically enhanced ass.

* * *

I needed boxes, packing tape. I was going to have to make a trip to the hardware store. I honestly didn't know if you were going to be working. When I walked in, you were ringing up a woman doused in denim who was purchasing lightbulbs. I looked at you, objectifying every inch of your body, though I don't think you noticed.

When you were done, you asked me if I needed any help. When am I ever going to get the chance to talk to you? I was tired of waiting, fantasizing, overstimulating my imagination. The encounter with your wife was awkward and uncomfortable and I was running out of time here. She may have even said something to you, outing my perversion.

"Do you have any boxes you're getting rid of? I'm moving."

"We just broke a bunch down. But you can check in the back, maybe by the Dumpster."

"Can you come with me?" You could have said no. I could have found them myself. But you followed.

"You live on my street."

I nodded and smiled and blushed.

"I see you watching me."

If I had breasts, they might have collapsed at that moment, exploded upon the impact of your breath on my skin.

"I wasn't sure if you noticed."

"Tell me why you watch."

"First tell me why you fuck yourself so often. I met your wife. She's—"

"I'm sure you know firsthand: if you want a job done right, then you might as well do it yourself."

"So then you prefer *your* hands to someone else's?"

"I'm at work. I can't do this now."

I grabbed as many boxes as I could carry and began walking

away, severely disappointed, though I'm not sure what I had
been expecting to happen.

"You need help? I can carry these boxes to your car."

"I didn't drive. But I only live a few blocks away."

"Let me ask my boss if I can leave for a few minutes."

"Oh, it will take longer than that."

We are walking to my house, our hands entertained by boxes
and my eyes absorbed with what I know is inside your pants.

I drop the boxes on my porch so I can unlock my door. You
follow me in.

"Where you heading?"

"New York."

"Alone?"

"With my boyfriend."

"I have fifteen more minutes."

You drop all the boxes you were carrying, a lot more than I
was. Sweat drips down your forehead and I ask you if you need
a cloth or something cold to drink.

"I have fifteen more minutes," you repeat. "You know what
I want."

I don't think about my boyfriend while you unzip your jeans
and pull them down a bit awkwardly. Your boxers are crumpled
and torn. You have more hair than I thought you had. I'm not
judging, just noticing. I grip your dick and squeeze hard enough
to push a sound out of you, a grunt or muffled breath. It is
thicker than I expected, which is a pleasant surprise. It is sweaty
and tired and curious and uncircumcised. My tongue pushes
itself out from between my lips and spreads itself along the
ridge of your dick. My spit mixes with your sweat, creating a
salty, cherry-flavored marinade. I lick your cock in long, heated
strokes. Up and down, drizzling my taste buds along the sides of

you. I love how expressive a dick can be. I grow jealous of your erection, wishing I could produce one of my own.

You are fucking my mouth as I push my fingers inside my underwear and finger my clit, flicking away at my miniature erection. You expand in my mouth as I suck on skin cells left there by your hand. For a moment, I wonder if your hand is jealous, realizing how much better I am at making you come.

Come. Come. Come.

My teeth retreat while I suck and blow and lick and hum over your cock. You arch your back, silently informing me that you are about to—

Come. Come. Come, my tongue demands.

You try and push away, but I want all of you. My cheeks feel swollen and tired, desperate for completion and the power of your cock claiming my throat. I want to know what you taste like.

When you come, will it taste similar to Costella, with its rich seasoned flavor, or more like top sirloin with its garlic infusion and rusty aftertaste?

After you came, your dick retreated back into its plaid boxer shell and you wiped away your remaining come with your fingers and dried them on your pants. It wasn't supposed to be romantic or end in an embrace. We never kissed and I still don't know your name.

ORCHID

Jacqueline Applebee

I think I have the hots for Viktor." I adjusted my stockings and stepped out of the toilet stall. My best friend and fuck-buddy, Peggy, gawped at me. "The new guy? Viktor from Accounts?" I nodded. "Viktor with the long brown hair?"

I sighed. Viktor had glossy hair and bright green eyes. He was a beautiful man.

"Hang on." Peggy dried her hands. "You cannot have a crush on Viktor. He's, you know…"

"He's Russian?"

"Not that." She poked me. "He's vanilla!" she finally blurted. "Wendy in Personnel dated him when he first started here. She told me all about him. Face it, Katie. He's vanilla, and you're a slutty submissive bottom."

"I know," I said with a sigh. "But vanilla folks need sexing-up, too."

"You can't date a vanilla guy, Katie. It's not natural."

"I can do whatever I want." I thought for a moment. "I can do whomever I want, too."

Peggy shook her head. "Would you even know what to do with him?"

"I'll find out," I said weakly. "I'll look it up on Wikipedia."

Peggy was having none of it. "Raspberry ripple—that's what you are, Katie. Raspberry ripple with extra sprinkles and a chocolate flake. You won't have a snowball's chance in hell of getting off with him. Viktor will never look at a pervert like you."

"Gee, thanks." I tried to put it out of my head, but Viktor was like an itch I couldn't scratch away. I saw him everywhere, gazing down from his framed photo on the wall as employee of the month, standing in line in the cafeteria or chatting on the phone, his beautiful voice a melody to my ears. I didn't know why I wanted someone like him. He was nothing like the other men I'd been with, stern tops and domineering businessmen. Even the female security guard on the front desk would make me drool. But Viktor was different. He was soft spoken, considerate, and smart as all hell. Maybe it was his vanilla nature that made him so exotic to me.

I saw Viktor outside work one day after lunch. A few teenage boys were kicking a ball to and fro in the parking area. Viktor did a fancy move, intercepting the ball as he walked by. He balanced it on his head, and then balanced the ball on his chest. He twisted around, and then kicked the ball to the boys, who smiled and waved at him. Damn, he was good with children, too. Viktor was perfect.

Peggy walked by, watching me eye up my Russian. "No, Katie. Viktor is vanilla. He will not want to spank you. He won't know the first thing about restraint."

"Get lost. Stop bugging me."

"He's coming this way," she said, and then scampered off. "I'll be in touch," she yelled over her shoulder.

I swallowed as he walked toward me. I spun on my heels and

practically ran inside the building. I jabbed the elevator button, willing it to arrive quickly. But the elevator was not quick enough. I squeezed inside, and then I pressed the button for my floor. I looked up when I heard his voice from the foyer.

"Hold on." The door swished shut just as he stepped inside. I couldn't be in the same elevator as my fantasy guy; it was inhuman.

"Hello, Katie. Is that a new dress?" He sounded nervous, as if he was desperate to make conversation. Why would he be nervous with me?

I shook my head, desperately trying not to speak. I was sure my voice would come out with a stammer if I did. My mobile phone chirped to life. Peggy was on the other end.

"Viktor is vanilla," my friend hissed. "He will sneer at your crystal butt plug. He will never use a cane on your arse." I pressed the phone to my chest, silencing her chatter.

Viktor leant across me to press the button for his floor. "I was made employee of the month again," he said, looking almost embarrassed.

"I heard. That's three times in a row, isn't it?"

Viktor nodded. "The director gave me a special gift: tickets to see the *39 Steps* in Piccadilly Circus. I have two tickets."

I looked at him blankly.

"Would you like to come with me?"

"Vanilla!" I could still hear Peggy's voice. "He will laugh at your floggers. He will pour scorn over your spreader bars. Stay away from him."

I clicked my mobile shut, and then I looked at Viktor, smiling. "Sure, that sounds like a lovely idea."

Viktor grinned and exited the elevator. As soon as the door closed, I pressed Peggy's number. "Listen you crazy bitch, quit calling me. I'm not listening to you. I'm going to shag that pretty

Russian if it's the last thing I do!" I clicked the phone shut. The doors opened suddenly. Viktor was still standing outside. Had he heard me? I inwardly cringed. He must have thought I was absolutely mad.

There were positives of being out at work as a bisexual woman. I didn't have to dress up for the office. Most people seemed to think bisexual meant that I ought to dress like a whore. So, as a result, my black lace tops were as welcome as my microminis and my lip piercing. Straight people sure do think weird.

I got dressed for my date. I wore dainty earrings shaped like tiny coiled whips; they were too small to discern unless you got really close. I found a black dress that was short, but not scandalously so. I actually looked quite subdued.

The *39 Steps* was a hoot, of course. I especially liked the part of the play when the hero and heroine were handcuffed together, fleeing from the law through the Scottish Highlands. I wondered what it would be like to kneel in front of Viktor, hands shackled, eyes shut. My mobile vibrated against my lap; I knew I should have left it at home. I sighed when I saw that it was a text from my annoying friend. *Vanilla is vanilla*, it read. *He will never blindfold you.*

I started to feel a little down. Viktor and I went for a meal in Covent Garden when the play ended. I picked at my salad, but had no appetite.

"Are you all right, Katie?" Viktor asked.

"I'm fine."

"You look like something is on your mind." He squeezed my hand; it was heavy, solid. I shivered as I imagined that hand on my rear, spanking me hard and fast. It was never going to happen.

"I think I'd best go."

"Why?"

"I don't think this will work," I said pointing between the two of us.

"Is it because I'm Catholic?" Viktor asked, looking distressed. I shook my head. "Then it must be because I am Russian."

"You're vanilla, Viktor."

Viktor looked at me blankly. "I am white, of course."

I almost smiled at that. "Look, I enjoy being tied up. I like being ordered to suck cock." A waiter crashed into our table as I said that. He blushed furiously, and then backed away. "I mean, surely you have to know about me."

"I thought it was an office rumor, that people were being cruel."

"I don't think you'll like me if you get to know me. I'd rather be just friends, Viktor." It was a barefaced lie, but he was too gorgeous a person to lose completely.

"Let me make up my own mind about that, Katie." He held out his hand. "I am sure we can come to an arrangement that will be good for both of us." We walked outside and hailed a cab to his place near Finsbury Park.

"So if I am vanilla, does that make you strawberry?" he asked as we entered his building.

"Apparently I'm raspberry ripple with extra sprinkles and a chocolate flake."

"I still do not understand. Is vanilla an insult?"

I turned to Viktor on the threshold of his apartment. "I didn't mean it as one, but now that I think about it, vanilla could be taken that way."

Viktor kissed me lightly on the lips, the barest brush of his mouth on mine. "Vanilla is also a type of orchid."

"Really?" I hadn't heard that one before.

"It is a highly-prized flower that must be treated just so, or else the precious stamen will be lost." Viktor ran a finger over my breast. My nipples ached for him to squeeze them. "The sensuous fragrance is a well-known aphrodisiac, too."

My mouth hung open. I gulped as a thrill of desire shot from my tongue down to my clit. Viktor grinned at me, and then he led me inside, but instead of heading to his bedroom, he ushered me to the bathroom.

"I have never made love in this room before. It could be a not-so-vanilla experience for me, yes?"

"Sex in the shower? Sounds good." I stripped out of my clothes quickly, turned on the water, and got in. Viktor watched with eager eyes. I wondered what he'd make of the tattoos that ran down my back. "Aren't you going to join me?" I asked, enjoying the feel of hot water over my skin.

"You are rather nice to watch, Katie." Viktor stood with his hands covering his crotch. Poor soul, but he was a shy one. I actually started to feel quite turned on being naked in the sight of a fully clothed man. I squished my breasts together, stroked over my bottom and bent over to drape my fingers over my toes. I smiled when I heard Viktor's intake of breath.

"Let me dry you off." He held out a fluffy towel.

"Aren't you coming in?"

"I want you in my arms," he whispered. I sighed, but switched off the shower and stepped out of the tub. Viktor instantly surrounded me with the towel. He held me tight in a very strong embrace. I struggled a little, just to see what would happen, but he held me fast. Things were getting better and better. He kissed me, and this time his kiss was all consuming. I gasped, wriggling about in the towel. If this was what vanilla folks did, then I was over to their side like a flash.

"You are a very strange woman," Viktor murmured. "It arouses you to not be able to move?"

"That's right."

He pressed me to sit on the edge of the bathtub. "Then do not move now." He swept my legs open. The towel fell down around me. Viktor ignored it; he went down on his knees in front of me, and then he bent his head to my cunt. I willed him to kiss me there, but Viktor only breathed over my sensitive flesh.

"Please," I begged shamelessly. "Oh, please, Viktor." He grinned up at me. And then in an act of extreme sadism, he touched my clit with the barest tip of his tongue. I thrashed about like a crazy person, desperately pushing my whole crotch up to his face.

"I told you not to move," he whispered, and looked up at me. I took a breath, stilled. Viktor licked me again, tiny movements that were incredibly intense.

"This is torture," I hissed. "You're killing me!"

Viktor chuckled against my cunt. "Is this not exactly what you desire?"

I froze as I actually saw the lightbulb flash above my head. Viktor was right.

"You clever bastard!" I grunted.

"Now, now, it is not vanilla to swear during sex." He pushed a finger into my cunt, making slow deep movements. I wailed like a harpy. My clit throbbed. Viktor sucked on it, harder this time. I clutched at the back of his head and humped his face until I came noisily. The next time I saw Peggy I was going to give her a blow-by-blow account of how spicy this vanilla guy really was.

"Quite enthusiastic, aren't you?" Viktor wiped his face with the towel before he stood. I wrapped it around my hips and followed him out of the bathroom to his living room.

Viktor served me wine and strawberries. "No raspberries, I'm afraid," he said with a grin. "Although I am quite intrigued by the sprinkles part."

"Let me enlighten you," I said, and then I shimm
the towel to stand naked before him. "Will you take c
clothes?" Viktor did as I requested, though I'm such a su.
I hated to give him any instruction at all. Viktor sat dem __y
on his sofa, still covering up his hard erection. Finally he gave
up and removed his hands. His cock was pink and delicious
looking. I rummaged in my handbag for a moment, tossed him
an extra-strong condom and a sachet of lube. Viktor looked at
me quizzically for a moment before he rolled it on.

"Put the lube over the condom. I need you nice and wet for
me." As Viktor worked, I stood with my back to him. I planted
one foot on either side of his feet. I reached back, held on to his
biceps, and then I lowered myself down to sit. I could feel Viktor
try to direct his cock into my cunt, but I angled myself so his
cock prodded my asshole.

"Are you sure?" he whispered.

"You want to know about the sprinkles?"

"Yes."

"Then let me show you how sweet it can be."

Viktor grunted as I slowly lowered myself down. Inch after
inch of his length pressed inside me. I reveled in the way I
stretched around him, savored the deep penetration that I loved.
I didn't realize my eyes were shut until they fluttered open.

Viktor was rigid behind me. "Sprinkles," he whispered.
"Candy-colored sprinkles." He moved carefully, slowly, and
then he said something in Russian that I didn't understand. I
was all the way on him, impaled on my vanilla lover. I moved
forward a little and then back. Viktor hissed. I raised myself up
and then came down with a quick hard thrust. Viktor screamed.
In fact, the man screamed like a girl. He held me by the hips,
moving me up and down roughly. Every movement gave the
same response. He reached around to grab a cushion, and then

he shoved the corner of it into his mouth. I laughed as he gagged himself. I moved in a wild fashion, bouncing up and down on his cock, my arms flailing, my hips bucking. Viktor threw down the cushion and then he pulled me to him fully, holding me so tight that I could barely breathe. It was heavenly. His movements stilled, and then he sagged against me.

"I suppose this means I am raspberry flavored now?" Viktor asked in a weak voice.

"Don't sweat it, love," I soothed, patting his leg. "I think you've made me appreciate vanilla, too."

"We are an ice-cream sundae," he said, starting to chuckle against my back.

"A knickerbocker glory!"

"With plenty of sprinkles." He kissed my back.

"Topped off with hot fudge sauce," I replied with a laugh.

Viktor froze. "Maybe we can save the sauce for next time?"

I grinned. "To tell you the truth, I'm rather looking forward to you showing me how good vanilla can be." I eased myself up with a wince, and then collapsed in his arms.

"I will teach you about my style, and you will teach me about yours." He kissed my hot skin. "Do we have a deal?"

We shook hands. "You got it." I snuggled closer to his furry chest. "Next time I'll bring my ropes. We'll have a blast."

"You are joking with me, yes?" Viktor asked hesitantly.

"No."

My lover said nothing, but I could feel his cock stir. This would be the start of a beautiful friendship.

CHERRY
BLOSSOM

Kayar Silkenvoice

early or late
to fall is a joy!
cherry blossoms
—Kinko-jo, eighteenth century

I bumped into her in my *ryokan* in Kyoto. I smelled her exotic scent just milliseconds before my sleep-fogged brain registered the ledge I was supposed to step over in order to leave my suite—too late, of course. I tripped and fell to my knees like a penitent worshipper, one hand clutching the belt of her kimono, the other pressing down onto her foot. She staggered slightly, from surprise or the impact. I couldn't tell which, but I feared the latter.

"*Gomen nasai. Daijoubu desu ka?*" I stammered. *I'm sorry. Are you all right?*

My partner had taught me that phrase early on in the trip, after he tired of apologizing on my behalf to all the people I

bumped into. And I bumped into a lot of people as I was
constantly staring upward in astonishment at the cherry blossoms that seemed to adorn all of Japan.

Cool hands cupped my cheeks and tilted my head backward.
Dark eyes peered into mine, eyes so dark I could not distinguish
the pupils from the iris. "Are you hurt?" she asked me. Her
voice was typically girlish Japanese, but her accent was pure
Queen's English.

I gaped stupidly at her, a slow blush creeping up my torso
and flagging my cheeks. Humiliation burned through me, but
so did a peculiar excitement. I lifted my hand off her sandaled
foot, the foot clad in those white socks with the split toe that
had fascinated me since I'd first spotted them. I'd hoped to get
a close-up view one day, but this was hardly what I'd had in
mind. I released my hold on her *yukata,* a simple blue-and-
white *yukata* similar to the one I was wearing, and with her
help, I stood up.

"Are you certain you're not hurt?" she asked again in her
fluent English.

I watched her rosebud mouth shape the words, saw her fine
brows knit in that perfect oval face. Her skin was lovely, creamy
and golden, like custard. She smelled of flowers and herbs, a
concoction that was pungent enough to penetrate my daze. I
wanted to gather her up and press my nose to her skin, smelling
her everywhere. I was shocked with a fleeting mental image of
her splayed on the low table that our *kaiseki* feasts were served
on, and then my stomach rumbled, reminding me of why I'd
been stumbling out of my room.

Breakfast.

"I'm fine, really. There's nothing wrong with me that a cup
of tea won't fix. I need some caffeine. Too much sake last night,
you know..." I babbled groggily and blushed again. My voice

was so husky that I barely recognized it as my own. Too much sake indeed. The Gion District offered many late-night pleasures in addition to the geisha and their *maiko,* and my lover and I had partaken of them until nearly dawn. Thankfully, our *ryokan* did not have a curfew.

I smoothed my *yukata* over my pajamas and tucked a lock of hair back behind my ear, then smiled hesitantly at the woman I'd unintentionally accosted.

"Thank you for your help. I'm Sophie MacRae." I bowed slightly and withheld my hand, having noticed that the Japanese had a thing about hands. They washed them compulsively, especially before meals, and rarely touched hands if it could be avoided.

"Miyuki Futohara," she said, and bowed to me, her eyes downcast.

I was struck again by her beauty, by the music of her voice, the perfection of her skin and the symmetry of her features. I wanted to photograph her. I wanted to kiss her. But most of all I wanted to pull the decorative clips from her hair and run my fingers through it. I understood, with sudden clarity, how a woman's beauty could inspire poetry, and songs and even wars.

At that moment a young woman shuffled up to us. I recognized her as the innkeeper's daughter. She was plain compared to the other woman, but she looked serene in her traditional Japanese dress, including a pale pink *obi* that bound her from breasts to hips. She bowed to me and gestured.

"Your breakfast is ready, Miss," she spoke in halting English.

I blushed again, horrified. I wanted to groan, but I breathed out slowly instead. I was late, and the Japanese were sticklers about being prompt. Tardiness was considered disrespectful, if not rude.

I bowed to the beautiful Miyuki. *"Arigato gozaimasu."*

She bowed in acknowledgment of my gratitude, her poise enviable.

I bowed to the girl. *"Gomen nasai."*

As I followed the innkeeper's daughter, I wondered if it was wishful thinking on my part that Miyuki's eyes were following me. I stumbled again, feeling unsettled and breathless. My morning had gotten off to a rough start, but it wasn't anything that breakfast and a long soak in the *onsen* wouldn't fix.

My traditional Japanese breakfast was a filling mixture of a half-dozen small dishes that in many ways were indistinguishable from any other Japanese meal: boiled rice, steamed fish, miso soup and *nori*. The difference was mostly in the presentation, I think, with the ceramic dishes being more rustic in appearance. When I finished, I walked across the tatami mats, slipped into my sandals, and did my best to glide gracefully down the cobbled walkway to the bathhouse. I desperately needed a soak, and the *o-furo* tub in my room was a bit small for what I had in mind.

I entered the anteroom to the women's *onsen* and stripped down, placing my clothing in a basket. There was a woman there with her child, but I scarcely noticed them. In Japan, there is no such thing as body modesty, or at least, not in a form that Westerners would recognize. Entire families bathe together, and businessmen often soak together, enjoying the naked communion, the sense of sharing that comes when there is no possibility of concealment. But as casual as they seem about nudity, the Japanese are sticklers about cleanliness, and those using the communal baths must follow a strict code of hygiene. A Japanese friend of mine made sure to educate me on the bathing customs, so that I would not embarrass the attendants with the need to explain to the *gaikokujin* why she had to leave the *sento*.

There is something meditative about the bathing ritual, something as deeply sensuous as it is cleansing. I stepped under a showerhead and soaked myself, then sat on a little stool and slowly scrubbed from head to toe with a brush and soapy fingers. When every inch of me was pink and gleaming, I rinsed off, making sure there was no soap or shampoo residue. My skin tingled from the bristles of the brush, a tingle that bordered on pain but was a precursor of tingling to come. The water in the pool would be very, very warm.

Yukata wrapped back around me, I stepped into a pair of wooden sandals used exclusively by bathhouse patrons and passed through the doorway to the open-air *onsen,* or hot-spring pool. It was bordered by a high bamboo fence, tightly woven together, and surrounded with plants and stones that formed a garden I had meticulously cataloged in my mind for possible reproduction back home. The petals from the over-hanging cherry tree floated on the surface, looking like hot-pink confetti.

I stepped out of my wooden sandals, then removed my *yukata* and folded it neatly, placing it atop them. I stood for a long moment with my face upturned to the sky, enjoying the feel of the sun and the cool April air on my bare skin. And then I stepped into the petal-strewn pool.

I was prepared for the heat and still I gasped. It seemed to sear my skin. A wave of gooseflesh washed over me, making my nipples impossibly hard. Slowly, ever so slowly, I worked my way down into the pool, until water lapped at my collar-bones and the bubbles of air trapped around my hair follicles danced toward the surface like hundreds of tiny, teasing fingers. I fantasized about sharing the bath with Miyuki, my mind filled with images of small breasts bobbing in the water and tendrils of damp hair and cherry blossom petals clinging to her slender neck. I wanted to touch myself, wanted to slide my fingers into the slippery wetness of my pussy, and would have, if I hadn't known how it would have defiled the water in the eyes of its patrons.

I had the pool to myself and I enjoyed it fully, letting the images and sensations play over me and through me, allowing my imagination free rein with my impossible girl crush. I thought about my boyfriend, too, called back to Tokyo for a couple of days, leaving me without an outlet for my passion at a time when I desperately wanted a hard, fast fuck.

Eventually the hot water sapped my desire from me, and I floated on my back for a long while, watching the petals from the cherry fall willy-nilly and land sometimes on the water, sometimes on my skin. A poor attempt at *ku* drifted into my mind: *The tree's passion, spent / comes to rest / on my flesh.* The sounds of Kyoto wafted in, but they were pleasant, noninvasive, almost surreal. I knew I should go dress and resume exploring the city, but it wasn't until I felt light-headed that I moved to leave, and I had to do it by inches. I was so thoroughly relaxed, so limp and languid, that I felt like kelp struggling to crawl up out of the primordial sea.

A brisk shower under cold water soon cleared my head and firmed up my muscles. I put my pajamas back on and the *yukata* over them and was in the anteroom slipping into my sandals when a door opened. The sign on it had *kanji* symbols and the English word MASSAGE. A Japanese woman stepped out, bowed to someone inside, and then left. The door swung completely open and there was Miyuki. Seeing her standing there, my heart tripped over itself and landed at my feet. I had to walk past her in order to leave the bathhouse, and I wasn't sure my legs were steady enough.

"Would you like a massage, Miss MacRae?" she asked me in

that girlish voice that plucked some invisible strings inside me, making me quiver.

A massage? Dear god. I nearly swooned at the thought of her hands on my bare flesh. My knees forgot to support me for a split second, and I grabbed for the wall.

"Here, let me help you," she said, and wrapped an arm around my waist. My skin tingled where she touched. "Did you stay too long in the pool?"

I nodded, grateful for the proffered excuse for my weak knees. Her scent wove around me again, that potent herbal and floral blend, and I found it more intoxicating than sake. She guided me through the door and into the room, stopping before a shoji screen.

"Would you like an invigorating massage to give you energy?" she asked.

I struggled to find an excuse that would release me from the exquisite torture I knew I would experience under her hands, but the words did not rise to my lips.

"Um...sure, I guess. Yes."

Uncertain as to what I should do, I began undressing while she slid the shoji screen aside. Beyond lay a massage table and a window overlooking a lovely little pocket garden. She slipped off her *yukata,* revealing a plain cotton tunic and long expanse of bare legs. I nearly choked on the sudden flood of saliva. I wanted to push her back onto the padded table and feast on her, taste her, put to use those oral skills I'd developed at college. I took a deep breath to steady myself and tried to clear my mind of its inappropriate imagery. Miyuki waited patiently by the table until I approached, naked as the day I was born, and then she guided me to lie on my front.

Warm hands spread even warmer oil over my skin. Wave after wave of gooseflesh followed in the wake of her fingertips.

As her hands slid over my shoulder, I smelled that tantalizing scent and realized it was the oil. Mmmm. I definitely wanted some of that to take back home. Large quantities of oil were poured onto my skin and she spread it around with long, broad strokes of her tiny hands. It felt like she was an artist and the oil was paint and I was her canvas, longing for the brushes of her imagination.

"You have beautiful skin," she said. "So white, like milk."

As she leaned into me, pressing her palms along my spine, her upper thigh brushed rhythmically against my fingers, making them tingle. I found that I was holding my breath, wondering if it was intentional or not. Soon her hands glided down my back to my hips, to the largest erogenous zone on my body. She kneaded me there, making me delirious with the pleasure of her fingers sliding along my pelvis, her thumbs pressing deep into the muscles of my ass.

A long, low moan escaped me as her hands lifted and separated my buttocks. Cool air touched my secret parts, making me aware of how aroused I was. I felt a blush creep up my neck, burning my cheeks. I moaned again as she worked my thighs, her fingertips occasionally brushing my outer labia with fleeting touches. I was spared further mortification as her hands worked down my legs, squeezing and pumping my calves.

"Roll over please," she said, and I did so.

She placed a scented cloth over my eyes and draped another over my hips, and then she began working my feet. It felt wonderful. My poor feet had been pounding the pavement all over Kyoto as I made my way from one shrine to the next, and the feel of her fingers on the pressure points had me moaning and sighing within moments. Eventually her hands slipped up over my ankles, and with a few soothing strokes she soon passed my shins. When her fingers touched my thighs I was torn between spreading my thighs wide and fleeing the room. To my embarrassment, I was so aroused I could smell myself, even over the potent herbal oil that she dribbled on my skin from her cupped hands. It was exquisite, the hot droplets of oil hitting my skin, as erotic as wax play, and I heard myself moaning involuntarily.

Her hands glided up my quadriceps to my hip, then curved down over my inner and outer thigh on the downstroke. As her fingers fluttered against my outer labia, I gasped and jolted and moaned shamelessly. I was hopelessly, passionately aroused. My body pulsed with lust. I brushed aside the cloth and opened my eyes to see Miyuki looking down at me, a slight smile on her face. Her dark eyes seemed particularly intent. As she met and held my gaze, she slid her fingers deliberately along my labia until she was cupping my mound.

"Do you want a G-spot massage?" she asked me in her Queen's English accent.

She spoke so primly that it took a moment for what she was saying to sink in, and then I realized what she was asking. I blushed. The telltale redness started at my breasts and crept up my neck to my cheeks. I suddenly felt funny inside, all fluttery and tense. I'd heard about "happy ending" massages, but I'd never gotten one, and it certainly wouldn't have occurred to me to ask her for one. But since she was offering... *Oh no, I couldn't... Well, maybe...* My thoughts vacillated wildly, and then it occurred to me that I would always wonder what it would have been like to have this exquisite woman bring me to orgasm in this setting. I knew that I would kick myself for the rest of my life if I said no. So I nodded, not trusting myself to say even the word *yes* with any coherency.

Miyuki's smile deepened and then she turned away from me, only to return a moment later with cupped hands full of oil. Again, she dribbled oil over my skin, this time over my lower belly, mound and labia. It was a delicious sensation, and the slow slide of the oil droplets down my skin were maddening. Slowly, almost languidly, she spread the oil along my skin, and when she reached my bare mound her fingers probed gently, curling into me. I moaned, and to my embarrassment my hips bounced. She smiled at me and put a hand over my mouth, and then with a deft move, slipped her fingers into me.

I do not know what she felt when she slid between the folds and into my aching pussy, but what I felt was so intense, I wanted to scream. And I did. I lifted my hands and pressed hers across my mouth and screamed into it as she worked her other hand into me. Those deft little fingers wiggled and massaged until she worked them into me far enough to find my G-spot. When she curled those fingers up against that place and started rocking against it, I released her hand and grabbed the sides of the massage table instead.

Fuck! It felt so good! She knew what she was doing, jabbing her fingers up against my G-spot in a compelling rhythm that had me bucking and rocking. I felt the orgasm building, felt my pelvic muscles contracting, and she must have known I was close because her free hand tangled in my hair and my eyes opened to see her face lowering toward me. When her lips touched mine I came, came hard, ejaculating my breath into her, my body undulating and twitching as the movements of her hand slowly subsided.

When the kiss ended she looked into my eyes and smiled, and then took her hands away. I made a disappointed noise that was followed shortly by a gasp as she pulled her tunic over her head and shucked off her white panties. I only had time to notice that her pubic hair was straight before she was climbing onto the table with me and fitting herself between my thighs. And then she began the most insidious movements of her body, rubbing her hairy mound against my bare one, pricking my clit.

She lay fully on top of me and used the oil on my skin to slide herself back and forth, capturing my mouth for a kiss each time her incredibly pleasurable upward glide ended. Her tongue probed at my lips and they seemed to part of their own accord. Her tongue thrust into my mouth and her arm curled under my head, trapping me in a kiss that seemed to go on forever as our bodies rubbed together more and more frantically.

Seared by her kiss, I panted to catch my breath as she reared over me and started bucking her hips against mine. Jagged bolts of pleasure pierced me with each thrust of her mound. I grabbed her hips, digging my fingernails into her as my mind flew apart like paper cranes in a breeze. Every thought, every sensation focused on the pleasure pulsing through me as Miyuki jogged her hips against mine in a frenzy. Her hair came free and fell around us to form a curtain of black silk. It tickled and teased my face and chest as she pounded herself into me, mashing her clit against mine, and it was the feel of her hair flogging my nipples that pushed me over.

Every muscle in my body tightened. A massive orgasm roared through me. In a burst of euphoria, my fingers dug into her ass and pulled her up into me. I wrapped my legs around her thighs and bucked upward, grinding myself against her. She whimpered and cried out, her dark eyes wide and her mouth opened in a perfect O as she, too, climaxed with a staccato wail.

Sharp spikes of pleasure continued to jolt me as we lay tangled together on the massage table. I explored her body with my fingers, gently, as if she was the most delicate of cherry blossoms. Sliding my fingers through her hair, silken and heavy and impossibly thick, felt even better than I'd imagined. I cupped one of her breasts in my hand and played with the tiny nipple, making her gasp and rock against me, which sent even more jolts through me. I wanted more. I wanted a taste of her. I wanted to oil her up and explore her body as she'd explored mine. I wanted to... My euphoric thoughts were interrupted by a chiming sound.

Miyuki swung herself off the table. She grabbed a hand towel and started rubbing the oil off her skin. I sat up and looked at her.

"I have a massage in ten minutes," she said. "You will need to leave soon."

I felt her words like a blow to my stomach.

I must have made some pained noise because she stopped what she was doing and took my hand.

"This was not a normal massage hour. This was special," Miyuki said, giving my hand a slippery squeeze.

I smiled tremulously at her, aching for her, aching for the chance to make love with her again.

She must have read my mind, because she looked me in the eye and said words that made my heart soar. "I'll come to your room tonight, please."

Joy flooded me. I nodded through the tears that floated in my eyes like the petals of cherry blossoms drifting in the pond nearby. I wanted to get back to my room and ready it. There would be no need to venture out into Kyoto today. I was going to have my own personal cherry blossom viewing that night.

RAIN

Olivia Archer

M y husband is too lost in a rant about the upcoming elec-
tion to notice the rigid set of my body as I watch my best
friend kick off her shoes and place her legs in the lap of her
latest boyfriend, Rain. She waggles her red manicured toes and
asks for a foot massage. As Rain obliges, I imagine that I can
hear the rasp of his rough fingers rubbing her skin. Or maybe
I can feel them touching me—the way he did last Tuesday, the
first time we fucked.

The four of us are finishing liqueurs in our living room; my
lover is directly in front of me. His dark, curly hair and the
curve of his ass in those jeans tempt me, but I stare through
him, into the empty fireplace.

When I get up and clear some of the leftover dessert carnage
from the side tables, this gesture brings an end to the evening.
Marcy gathers her exquisite belongings, casually thrown on
the counter. I watch them go while standing in the foyer of
our so-called perfect little house. It took twelve years of our

lives to achieve this level of mind-numbing comfort.

Normally summer is my favorite season, but the warm night air wafting in doesn't provide its usual comfort. Instead, I'm reminded that the hillside surrounding our house, once verdant, is now parched and highly combustible, ready for a stray spark to set it ablaze.

"Jess, close the damn door," my husband yells from the next room. "What's gotten into you?"

Silence is my answer as I close the door on the night. My tongue is captured as I bite the tip, slowly and deeply, to keep the scream from surfacing.

He continues, oblivious. "Rain's turning out better than I'd expected. I had my doubts about him at first, you know, but it's an interesting change that Marcy's seeing someone with a little dirt under his fingernails. He's a man's man—I like that." Without even seeing him, I can hear the smirk on his lips.

"Yes," I venture. This one syllable is the most I can reply as I think of Rain's cock in my mouth, gagging me, teasing me; the smile I catch in his slate-blue eyes when I dare to look at him, when the four of us are together.

"We should invite them to the cabin this winter. Hey, if Marcy's still seeing him, that may be a record for her," he rounds the corner and catches me putting things away in the kitchen. "Leave that for the housekeeper! It irritates me to no end that you're always doing their job for them."

"Yes," I manage again. An answer to nothing, or maybe everything. My mind hinges on her toes. His fingers grazing Marcy's toe ring. The ring we bought together on one of our many shopping excursions when Rain was the latest one on her endless list, merely a name.

* * *

Rain was a rugged, artistic man who had moved to Los Angeles recently to work as the contractor on a high-end decorative mosaic tile project at a big-name hotel. Marcy, with her coiffed raven hair and designer suits, was "slumming it" with this nonprofessional and his calloused, creative hands.

Yes, Rain was just a name, an unusual name that Marcy always said with a bit of a laugh. I took no special interest until I met him and the air between us sizzled.

We had Marcy and her date-du-jour over for dinner every Friday night and would occasionally meet up around town on the weekend. The first time she brought Rain to the house he found me alone in the kitchen and helped get dinner together. He appeared to be a good cook since he jumped right in, easily assisting with the dishes I was preparing.

The men Marcy dated usually fawned over her sophisticated appearance, her powerful persona, and tended to agree with her strong opinions. Rain would calmly voice his views; he was a good conversationalist and could take on Marcy's sparring, but just as often, he chose to remain outside of the constant banter between her and my husband.

How Marcy and I became such close friends I still sometimes wonder—maybe the years had pulled us in different directions. When it comes to looks, she is all darkness and sharp angles, whereas I dress to display my hourglass figure and wavy blonde hair. She has always loved to debate and basks in being the center of attention; I would rather sit back and listen in, savoring my glass of wine.

After having dinner at our house for several weeks, Rain called me at work one Monday. His normally peaceful demeanor was absent as he awkwardly told me that he was very interested in me and thought the feeling was mutual.

He said he was taking a chance doing this, fearing I'd pull away, but he had to follow his instincts. He wanted more. He wanted me.

When I told him I thought he was crazy—how could we go there?—he paused a mere second, then told me there were outrageous things he fantasized about us doing together. I responded with stunned silence, absorbing every word, but too dazed to reply. He left it for me to think about.

In a few minutes, Rain had moved our physical attraction and comfortable friendship into a realm of sensuality that I didn't think could exist for me again; the boundaries that I believed to be immovable suddenly wavered with his words.

Every day that week he called at ten, a busy time at my office. I listened, immobile with the knowledge of where this could lead. *Do I quench the thirst in my soul?* I had no answer, so I kept absorbing his sexy words.

By Tuesday and Wednesday my panties were damp as I squirmed in my office chair.

When I missed his calls on Thursday and Friday because of meetings, he left messages, hot, explicit messages about how he was going to fuck me slowly, detailing each lick, each groan. I could imagine him jerking off as he spoke, throaty, horny. I replayed his messages a dozen times each day before deleting them from my work phone.

By the time I saw him with Marcy that Friday night, I was too turned on to look at him, afraid I'd betray my raw lust in front of everyone. He played it cool, until we had a moment alone, then stripped me naked with a glance and leaned slightly against me while we worked together in the kitchen. The energy between us was tangible.

His calls continued the next week. I fantasized about the scenarios he was describing, too shy to verbalize my desires just yet, and reorganized my schedule to be available for his timely phone call.

Midweek, when he told me he would tie me up, I closed my office door and confessed to him how I liked the cuffs to be tight enough to mar my skin. That I wanted to be gagged, blindfolded; led within a heartbeat, a breath, of a mind-blowing climax—and left hanging on the edge, until my partner allowed me to freefall into that pool of pleasure.

Our dialogues meshed seamlessly, and I spent many waking and sleeping moments hot for him in the summer heat. I dug out the old bullet vibrator and packed it in my car, getting myself off on the way to work as I thought about my next phone call with Rain.

At our house that Friday, he caught me by myself in the dining room to say that he wanted to take it to the next level, we had to meet up somewhere, he was going crazy like this. I said we couldn't. How could we? This wasn't adultery, yet—not really.

Rain didn't call me at work on that following Monday; I watched ten o'clock come and go, as I sat alone in my office trying to distract myself from my need.

On Tuesday, he called and told me that he would be downstairs in the lobby of my office building the next day at exactly ten a.m. I could be there, or not.

I met Rain in the most secluded corner of the lobby to ask him what the hell he thought he was doing here. He looked at me with that smile playing in his eyes while he discreetly showed me a room key to the hotel down the street where he was working.

My justification for going with him that day was to speak to him in a private place and let him know it was over, what we'd done wasn't even the beginning of what I wanted, but I should set a limit. Shouldn't I? Anyway, I had to be back in an hour to facilitate a conference call.

That call happened without me. The room was in an empty wing of the hotel. Once we were inside, he told me to phone my secretary and say I had a personal emergency. I did. It was so easy, I instructed her to send in the new guy. My body's every cell longed for Rain; if anything in my life had ever qualified as a personal emergency, this was it.

We kissed and caressed for a few moments before he slowly undressed me, neatly placing my items of clothing across a chair. From a tote bag he removed a beautiful garment: sheer, lavender. I could smell the warmth of the silk in the close closed-in summer heat of the room.

Standing naked in front of this stranger, my body felt electrified by the way he admired me. With my nose up against the collar of his dusty T-shirt, I could feel the rhythm of his blood beating in his tanned neck. My fantasies lined up in my mind as I absorbed Rain's essence.

His lips brushed my blushing cheek as he slipped the gown over my head and stretched its formfitting shape along my curves. The fabric hid nothing, accentuating the rise of my rose-colored nipples, clinging to the cleft of my mound.

He sat me in the other chair and removed a blindfold from his jeans pocket. "May I?"

My brain whirled through everything Marcy had told me about him, scanning for the mention of any red flags. Rain rated in the eightieth percentile on Marcy's spreadsheet of sexual conquests. The word she used was burned in my brain: perfunctory. They'd had sex twice, to finish off the evening, then he went home. She joked that he wasn't quite "wham, bam, thank you, ma'am" but he wasn't far from it, and she wrote off his disinterest as brooding artist's temperament.

"Why me?" I asked Rain. "Why this, why not her?"

"This connection between us, call it what you want, but you feel it, too. It's amazing, and I need more."

"I don't want an affair—I'm not that kind of woman."

Rain looked down at me, wrapped in his gossamer gown, and sighed. "Jess, your body seems to remember what kind of woman you are, what kind of woman you want to be again."

With that, he kissed my mouth, once, for far too brief a moment. Then he placed the blindfold over my eyes, cloaking my sight and unleashing my mind.

Seconds later, the sting of cool leather snapped against my thighs, making me jump. I grabbed his arms, feeling their wiry muscles and the slickness of his sweat.

Rain whispered, "Stay in that chair or I'll tie you to it," as he caressed me with what felt like a riding crop, pressing the silky fabric of the dress into the wetness between my legs. "For these moments, you are mine."

The tip of his leathery implement continued its exploratory path, setting my nerve endings afire. My body and mind moaned a response that said, *Yes, yes, yes...but who are you? The man that Marcy can't see, or the one that I can't forget?*

From behind, he hooked his arm around my neck, forcing my chin up and thrusting his tongue into my mouth, consuming my lips with a hunger I echoed in my veins. Rain had nothing to lose; he was an interlude in our lives. I was placing my relationship with my best friend on the line. Marcy was the girl who went through school with me, who'd helped me obtain all my clichés: the right college and Mr. Right. She still told me her secrets and knew mine. Until now.

This affair could jeopardize, destroy, implode my enviable marriage. My address in the best school district for our childless household. The ideal husband. A man who tells me he loves me

at all the right places in the conversation. A man who has never
fucked me until I held onto consciousness with only the thinnest
thread. Satiating sex was something I gave up: For marriage.
For stability, opportunity, upward mobility. Because I thought
that's how it worked in the world. Until Rain.

Rain released his forearm from my throat and captured both
of my nipples in his hands. He suckled the gossamer fabric that
clung to my breasts, the hot wetness pulling me deeper into the
abyss where only need resides.

His thumb opened my mouth but then left my lips hungry
as he unzipped his jeans. The velvety tip of his cock entered my
mouth in one thrust, scraping against my teeth and catching me
by surprise. The taste of him was an extension of the animal
electricity that he exuded. I salivated, unashamed, each drop
igniting a path of awareness as it slid down my face and dripped
onto my body.

For an eternity, I was untethered from this place and time;
he fucked my face. My eyes were unseeing, my mind numbed
to everything but the sensation of his cock sliding in and out of
my mouth. The diaphanous dress was damp everywhere from
my juices, my sweat. The room was pulsing with our carnal
energy.

The sound he made when he came was primal and I swallowed it, echoed it, deep in my cells.

He removed the blindfold and kissed my unseeing eyes as the
lids fluttered open in their newfound freedom. "I want you to
wait to come until we meet again. I'll tell you when," he whispered in my ear, then gave my ass a squeeze as we went to clean
up in the bathroom.

I had to pry myself away, the need to be quenched was so
enormous. Giving him one last lingering kiss, I stashed the dress
in my briefcase and returned to the office for the remainder of

the day. All the things that normally irritated me slipped off my
skin as I floated through the next few hours on a cloud.

My husband's voice carries into our tastefully decorated master
bathroom, "Don't sit in that hot water too long, you know how
it flares up your skin."

I should answer that I want him to come in here and do things
to me that he would be too ashamed to even think of. Things
I've hinted at, things I've asked for. Things he says he's done
to other women: When he was young. When he was "experimenting." But his cock will never bury itself in my ass. His nails
have never raised lines down my back. He says he believes in
forever and the sanctity of holy matrimony, the shining band of
gold. Somehow marriage to him is incongruous with the kind of
sex that is fucking. Making love is what we do. Making love in
a marriage that has lost love—*that* seems incongruous to me.

Could he fathom that a stranger had gnawed into my soul?
The man he's met a few casual times? The one he immediately
assessed as his inferior?

Rain has forged a path through the barbed wire of my mind.

I had upheld our marital monogamy, even though my
husband had his dalliance, once—supposedly. Early on.

But, of course, it meant nothing, and we did the obligatory
therapy, counseling.

Experts predict your marriage will be stronger if you can
weather an affair. We weathered. I withered even with the
weekly bouquet of flowers that adorns our table. Whether or
not they are spent, he throws them out and brings home a new
bunch, bearing them with a smile, a symbol of his supposed
fidelity, adopted after the affair and kept up all these years.
To show his fidelity to the wife he knows only as faithful, the
woman he expects will bear him children once her career is in

the right place, once we have advanced into the next income bracket.

But I keep taking the Pill.

And now, do I choose to throw my world away? Like my husband will toss out the half-spent roses when the bouquet on the table merely begins to fade, before petals wither, fall, touching the tablecloth with their dying imperfections.

My dalliance will contort the pastel-colored rooms of his mind.

Rain. This unknown man I've known mere moments, what will happen after he quenches the passion that rages silently within? Will my smoldering soul be extinguished, or will this essential part of me reignite?

How can I even think to say good-bye to my husband when, in the past twelve years, when was *I* ever really here? The person he slept beside and lived with was what he expected, what he neglected. His perfect wife.

His perfect wife is perfectly perverse.

I waited for Rain to tell me that I could get off. But he said everything except that, teasing me when I asked him if I could do it while we were on the phone together. Days passed as I burned slowly with this pent-up ecstasy. The only thing I could think about was release. And Rain.

Seeing him the following Friday with Marcy, hearing about him—it was almost beyond what I could bear; segments of my days were lost. I read Marcy's emails, listened to her on the phone, watched her face. She was the same—disinterested, even. How could she be Rain's lover and feel nothing?

When he finally beckoned me, it was not with a call, a text, an email. The four of us grabbed a quick Saturday lunch, on a sunny day, at a trendy place. At the end of the meal, Rain picked

up the check and counted out some bills while we were still at
the table. As we rose to make our way to the cash register, he
paused and casually asked if I would mind paying while he used
the facilities. Before I could answer, he placed the money in my
hand, and left.

The three of us went to the register together, with Marcy
talking on about her new client who promised big sales. The
corner of a piece of paper was visible below the bills. I slipped
the note into my purse before paying the cashier.

I didn't look then but paid and excused myself to the bathroom as well, hoping Marcy would not follow. Passing Rain, I
shot him a flustered look; his eyes didn't meet mine, but I could
see a smile playing at the edges of his lips.

In the bathroom, I went into the open handicapped stall and
stood there, reading his note. It said, "Make an excuse so we
can be alone five minutes from now."

No way. My mind reeled. No way in hell. We were headed
back to our respective cars and parting ways. There was no way
I could hook up with him now.

I tore up the note and flushed it. Watching the pieces swirl
down the bowl, it felt as if I was drowning the sin boiling in my
skin.

The three of them were standing on the sidewalk outside the
restaurant. My husband, impatient, gave me a glance that told
me he was ready to get out of here. We had tickets for a matinee
play and lunch service had taken longer than planned.

Marcy had her arm linked through Rain's and they were
stepping in the direction of their parked car. We all said good-
bye and began walking in opposite directions. With each step
my heart raced. *Five minutes,* his words said. I was counting the
seconds, willing them to go by and be past.

My husband was walking at a good clip and didn't notice at

first that I'd stopped. When he did, asking what was wrong, I told him lunch was not sitting well and that I needed to use the bathroom again. His face flushed with the beginning of anger, he said, "Do you want me to complain to the manager? Was it that fish?"

"No, no. I think it's nerves from all the pressure at work this week. I'll be fine. Meet me at the car, don't stand around in this heat. I'll be back as soon as I can."

Without waiting for a reply, I walked as fast as my strappy sandals would allow, straight back into the bathroom. I was alone and stood there, looking at myself in the mirror of this poshly decorated room and admiring the burnished bronze fixtures and floating sink bowls.

What now? I wondered as I paced the room. Our waitress entered; I forced a smile and went to the large, handicapped stall.

I sat down quietly on the edge of the toilet seat, listening to her noises a thin wall away. She was all business and finished in a minute. Feeling like a fool, I stood and the electric sensor flushed the empty toilet. As I began to exit the stall, I was startled as Rain rushed in through the door.

His beautiful eyes stood out in sharp contrast to the dark-chocolate color of his V-neck T-shirt. He laughed and pushed me back into the stall. Locking the door, he turned me so that I faced the far wall, my hands up against the tiles.

"Don't say a word, just feel me, and let yourself come," he whispered in my ear with a scratch of his stubble against my cheek.

As he knelt behind me, I could hear myself panting from the thrill of our riskiness. With his strong, tanned arms he roughly separated my legs, then gathered the thin fabric of my silk skirt in his hand and tucked it into the waistband to expose my damp panties. My ears pricked as I heard a door open, but it was someone entering the men's room next door.

Rain pulled my pink satin panties down, and I waited in tingling anticipation. A moment later I heard a click and a rip. I looked down between my legs and saw that he'd slit the crotch of my underwear open with his pocketknife.

He urgently pulled my panties back up and slid his tongue through the slit his knife had made. With his face pressed into me, there was no beginning to where we ended. I could feel every inch of his tongue as I clenched around him, my face against the cool tile wall. He fucked me with his mouth and I moaned with pleasure. My every nerve ending was awakened.

"Jess, shhhh." His warm breath exhaled against my back. I had to quell my disappointment that his tongue was no longer inside of me, but he quickly filled me with several fingers. They slid into my wet, aching sex where they belonged.

Holding me against him for stability, he worked his fingers inside me, jacking me off as I tried to suppress the panting, wild ecstasy that filled me. His thumb fluttered my clit and sent me over the edge. I came fast and hard, a lightning bolt of pleasure, followed by reality as he pulled down my skirt.

I turned to face him, wanting more. My hands brushed through his unruly shoulder-length brown locks.

"Please fuck me, Rain," I whispered, while stroking his hard-on.

"I will, but not now."

"What, are you going to go home with Marcy and fuck her?" My feelings for my best friend turned to anger as I pictured Rain mounting her with his cock, the cock that I still had not even seen.

"No, Jess, I'm not." Hurt flashed in his eyes. "Don't go there. You're not exactly sleeping alone at night. Let's get out of here before someone notices. There will be more, I promise."

My question of "When?" went unanswered; pleasure and pain wrestled within me. He pushed me out the door of the stall and locked it behind me. In the mirror, a flushed, rumpled version of myself reflected the confusion I felt but there was no time now for this. I washed my hands and splashed some water on my face. The wrinkled skirt would have to stay that way.

Walking quickly back through the restaurant and toward the car, I saw Marcy talking to my husband, who was smoking and pacing.

"Wow, you look like you've got a fever," she said. "You should skip the play and go home until whatever you have works its way out of your system."

I feigned a smile of thanks and dropped into the passenger seat.

My husband got in and asked if I wanted to go home.

"No, I'm fine. Let's go."

Though I'd been looking forward to the performance, it passed before my unseeing eyes as I recovered from the storm that was raging within me.

Marcy called me at work the following Friday morning to tell me that she'd be over for dinner, but had to leave early. And that she was bringing Walter, instead of Rain.

"What?" I asked, amazed.

"Well, Rain's on his way out of town, and you remember Walter, he's the CFO at that administrative firm. Anyhow, I've got to make it a short night and if I bring Walter—"

I interrupted her midsentence. "What? He didn't tell me he was leaving!"

"Who, honey, Rain? I just found out this morning when he texted me. He's going to Vegas to check something out. Anyhow, it wasn't going anywhere with us." I held my breath, waiting for her to put it together, to respond to my exclamations, to tell me she'd noticed a strand of my long blonde hair adorning his T-shirt or jeans. She paused a moment, then continued with more about Walter.

My mind raced. No more Fridays with Rain. In a way it was a relief because Rain and I had taken too many chances. If he continued to come over, we would probably get tipsy one night and end up fucking in my bathroom while Marcy and my husband debated politics. I didn't want to keep going in that direction.

As Marcy was saying good-bye, I heard the muted beep of my phone, alerting me to a new email. My heart raced when I looked at the screen. It was from Rain.

His message said, *I'm in Vegas for the weekend. Sorry to leave suddenly. Got an offer that I had to see to believe, doing Botticelli's* Birth of Venus *for a fountain at the premiere hotel. It'll be an incredible piece of art. Join me.* Attached was a ticketless confirmation in my name for a 10:45 flight to Vegas. That night.

Join me. Two simple words carried such weight. I sent him a response, congratulating him on his job and saying I didn't see how I could get away on such short notice. The words felt inadequate, dismissive. He'd put my feet to the fire; I jumped away before I would get burned.

The day passed by, as did the evening—with Walter, and not Rain. My husband was a bit disappointed at first, as he'd considered Rain as interesting a diversion as Marcy had. I was distracted, asking myself if I believed that, too; if I should just appreciate that he had reawakened essential parts of my being, but stop seeing him.

Marcy and Walter begged off before we'd even cleared the dinner plates from the table. I offered to pack dessert, but they both declined. So I sat at the dining room table savoring a cup of hot tea and my homemade biscotti while my husband went upstairs to watch some TV before calling it a night. It was just nearing nine.

After washing my dishes, I retrieved the note I'd typed at work from my briefcase and left it propped up against the fresh flowers on the table, to explain—as best I could. Then I walked out through the foyer of my perfect little house. And caught that flight to Vegas.

THE HAN

Justine Elyot

'm offering you a choice," he says, and I know exactly what comes next. "We can do this the easy way or the hard way."

The script is so familiar. In my three years as duty solicitor at the Maiden Street police station, I've heard Detective Sergeant Blake utter this phrase countless times. Sometimes whichever random villain I'm representing will choose the easy way—he or she will spill the beans, confess all, finger the Mr. Big behind the operation, and then Blake will smile his earnest smile, reassure them that it will be okay, pat them on the shoulder while they gibber about witness protection. Far more often, they plump for the latter option, in which case Blake has to bring out the big guns. Of course, I don't mean that literally. Blake's arsenal is wholly psychological, but it is no less deadly for that. An implication here, a tut and a shake of the head, a casual mention of a family member or acquaintance—I have seen all of these reduce a strong man to a crumpled, tear-stained wreck. He has mastered the art of being both good and bad cop simul-

...eously, and I cannot help admiring him for it. More than admiring. Desiring.

So which will it be? Easy or hard? The rules are a little different tonight. I do not preside over some sulking youth in a hoodie; there is no set of tattooed knuckles next to mine on the table. Indeed, there is no table. There is Blake and there is me, and we are on a bed. The situation has changed, as has the dynamic, but the question remains.

I push back my shoulders, lift my chin, meet his eyes.

"Make it hard," I tell him.

He smiles, his eyes firing, his ego challenged.

"You've never been easy," he says. "I just hope you know what you're letting yourself in for."

I think I do. God knows, I've studied the man long and hard. Three years of watching him, long legs pacing, fingers stroking chin, eyes distant with calculation, while I count down to the spring, the trap, the coup de grâce. I have learned to expect it, but the suspects never do; they are always caught off guard. They don't know that little quiver of cheek muscle, the slow tumble of hair over his brow, the impatient tap of forefinger that comes before the moment of doom. I know all of it intimately now.

I've also savored the gently intensifying wall of attraction between us that has grown up, brick by brick, with each interview. When he is the interviewing officer, I pay that extra bit of my attention, and when I accompany the suspect into the room, his eyes crinkle and the sides of his mouth twitch up. He teases me; there is subtle flirtation and the odd accidental brush of hands. I never thought anything would come of it, though, until tonight.

He is staring through the window, his back to us as I enter the room with Ginger, a shambolic teenager who seems almost more addicted to bungling shoplifting raids than he is to heroin. Blake's partner, Viv, opens the interview, switching on the recorder and speaking into it. "Interview started at twenty-one fifteen," she says, pulling out a seat for me.

Throughout the brief and unchallenging interview, Blake says nothing, brooding over at us from the side of the room. Viv handles the questions alone, negotiating a quick falling-apart-at-the-seams from a hapless Ginger and ending up with a confession.

"Thanks," says Viv, nodding briskly at me and escorting Ginger from the room. I stand to leave, unsettled by Blake's peculiar demeanor, but my movement finally precipitates speech from him.

"Stay," he says.

"Stay? Why?" I let myself sink back into the molded plastic. "Are you okay, Detective Sergeant?"

"You can call me Ben," he says.

"After all these years..."

"It's Ellen, isn't it?"

"Yes. Listen, I should..."

"You should. I should. We should. I've had some news tonight. I wanted to share it with you."

He comes to sit opposite me, swooping down and clasping his fingers. I can see that his eyes are burning blue. Whatever it is, it's firing him up.

"So then?" I open. The toe of his shiny black work shoe nudges my patent pump.

"I've been promoted. I'm DI Blake now. Detective Inspector."

"Congratulations."

"Thanks." His grin is vulpine. His foot inches forward until our calves rub together. "The promotion involves a transfer.

I'm leaving Maiden Lane. I'll be based at Stafford Row from now on."

"Oh." I can't conceal the falling of my face. "I'll miss you."

"I was hoping you would." His face is close to mine, the tip of his beaky nose blurring out of focus, his eyes still glassy-brilliant as ever. "I'll miss you, too. But we won't work together anymore, so…"

"So?"

"So…this." He darts forward and his lips touch mine. It's a whisper of a kiss, no more than a promise really, but it rocks me sideways. He hooks a leg around mine, capturing it. "If you want."

"I do want. Yes. I think I do."

He pushes my notebook aside and scoops up my hands until they are cocooned within his, held tightly inside, clenched into heart shapes.

"Are you going to interview me?" I ask with a low laugh, suddenly absurdly nervous.

"Interview you?" he says, kissing the captive hands. "Interrogate you. Put you under pressure. Make you sing like a canary."

"Here?"

He uncoils, releases me, throwing his head back and blinking at the ceiling, as if he can't quite believe what he's doing or saying.

"No, of course, not here." He snaps back to life, his lip curled in erotic challenge. "Where then?"

"Not my place, I'm afraid. I'm having an extension built; it's chaos. Dusty chaos."

"My flat then. It's not far."

He helps me from my chair and pulls me in close, bumping foreheads.

"You lawyers are a slippery lot," he murmurs. "But you aren't. Are you going to slip through my fingers?"

"I don't think there's a legal precedent," I tell him, intoxicated by his scent. "I'll let myself be guided by you."

"You do that."

On the short drive to his docklands apartment, we talk haltingly, as if we have only just met and picked each other up. Despite the three years of professional involvement and mutual attraction, we are strangers.

"Did you always want to do this?" I ask him.

"Oh, yeah." He flicks his eyes away from the darkened streets to meet mine with an abashed smile. "I had to train myself not to check you out all the time I was questioning suspects. I had to pretend you were some old scrote with a boil on the end of his nose, otherwise the thieves would have run rings around me."

"That's so strange." I am hugging myself, thrilled at this disclosure. "You know, I've felt the same way. For a very long time."

He turns the corner and drives down a ramp to an underground parking lot.

"Good," he says.

We make it to his front door in a shuffling tango, bodies intertwined, lips clashing, before falling through into the hallway. We half stagger, half crawl to the bedroom, landing on the bed in an urgent heap, ready to fulfill the night's promises.

"DS Blake. Ben." I snatch a second of lip freedom to speak his name.

"What? Don't talk. Keep kissing. Get your clothes off."

"I want you to..."

He pulls at my blouse, stretching the buttons to their limits.

"What? Name it. I'll do it. Just as soon as you're naked."

"Interview me."

He is taken aback by this; his fingers freeze and then retract from my buttons and he lies back on one elbow, surveying me as he would one of his more dangerous malcontents.

"What? Interview you?"

"Yes. I love your technique. It turns me on."

His chuckle starts off bemused then turns wicked halfway through.

"Yeah? You like that, do you? Like to be grilled?"

"I think you have a way about you. It's very masterful. Professionally and sexually."

"Masterful, eh? I suppose you'll want me to get the cuffs out then."

"Well, I...wouldn't object." I worry that I have said too much. He will write me off as a deviant freak.

But his playful demeanor is unchanged as he leans back to scrabble about in a bedside cabinet.

"You keep them in the bedroom!"

"Of course. Where else?"

We are singing from the same hymn sheet. Hallelujah.

He sits back up, dangling shiny metal chain-linked cuffs in front of my face.

"Let's be having you then," he says.

I offer him my wrists. He traces their veins with a caressing fingertip, reducing me to an essence of desire, before suddenly closing his fist around them and snapping the bracelets locked behind my back.

"Oh dear, oh dear, oh dear," he breathes. "What have you been up to, Ms. Carrington? I never thought I'd see you here. Anything you need to get off your chest?"

He flicks at the blouse buttons so that the top two slide open. Beneath the white silk, my chest and collarbone rise and fall against his hand.

"I've been set up," I tell him. One finger slips inside the silk and strokes the slope of a breast.

"Oh, I know, love. They framed you. You're innocent. I've heard it all before, a thousand times. But the evidence says otherwise, doesn't it?"

His sorrowful smile looks so genuine. It always does. He always looks as if the felon's fall from grace is breaking his heart.

I jut out a lower lip. "I didn't do it, officer."

He takes my chin in a hand, leans down to kiss the lie from my lips.

"Yes, you did," he says. "I'm offering you a choice. We can do this the easy way or the hard way."

The frisson that sizzles from my throat to my groin is strong, very strong. I am wetter than wet; I want to moan with need, to throw back my neck and invite him to plunge down and take me.

I push back my shoulders, lift my chin, meet his eyes.

"Make it hard," I tell him.

He smiles, his eyes firing, his ego challenged.

"You've never been easy," he says. "I just hope you know what you're letting yourself in for."

He puts a hand on my shoulder, holding me still, while he forcefully unfastens the rest of my blouse buttons, letting the silk swing open over my breasts. When it is untucked from my skirt, he rests his palms at the sides of my rib cage and puts his lips on my ear.

"You asked for it."

One hand slaps the seat of my skirt; I jump, as far as it is possible to jump when one is on one's knees, and yelp.

"Is that hard enough?" he asks. "Confess, or there's more where that came from."

"Ooh, I didn't do it!" I gasp, needing to feel that incendiary crack of palm against rump again. Did it really feel that good? I need backup data.

Backup data arrives on cue. The slow burn radiates outward across the curve of my ass. It really did feel that good. It felt better.

"Oh, come on," he whispers. "You don't expect me to believe that, do you? I've seen the charge sheet. You stand accused of stiff nipples." He pulls down my bra cups. The evidence stares him in the face.

"It's not how it looks," I insist stubbornly. Another gloriously loud smack reverberates off the lined cotton.

"What do you call this then?" He begins to roll the fat pink buds between ungentle fingers, flicking at them with the tip of a nail, examining them in excruciating detail, even putting his lips to them and blowing. *Oh. That feels good. Do it again.*

He straightens up, eyebrow cocked. "Well?"

I want to sob with disappointment. "It's just a physiological reaction...to the room temperature."

"My ass," he says, but it's *my* ass that gets another spank, harder than the preceding three, causing me to fall forward and land against his chest, my face crushed into his white cotton shirt. "The room's warm, Ellen. But your nipples are behaving as if they've been dipped in ice." His hand fixes itself in my hair, gently tugging at the roots. "What's that all about, eh?"

"Ask forensics," I mutter into his chest.

He laughs out loud and spanks me again.

"I think I need to step this examination up a level."

My blouse comes off, at least as far as the cuffs, beyond which it cannot travel, then my skirt zipper is dealt with and the protective material abandons my bottom and thighs, leaving them all the more open to Blake's merciless techniques. He lays me down on my back, so that he can remove the garment completely. While he's about it, he takes off my shoes, so that I lie in just a no-cup bra, knickers and stockings. I always wear stockings when Blake's on duty. Finally, it has paid off.

I pretend to cower when he straddles me, fully suited and ready for the kill, his tie falling into my face. Behind my back, the handcuffs are uncomfortable, but I can't bring myself to care. I am too busy trying not to fling my legs wide and beg him to mount me there and then.

"So we've established that your nipples are hard," he recaps, using his fingers to determine that this remains the case. It does.

"And I also note that your throat and collarbone are flushed," he says with a grin. "What do you think that tells me?"

"Hot," I say. "Heat."

"Oh, now the room has heated up, has it? From its previous arctic temperature? Come on." He brushes the backs of his fingers under my chin, down the line of my neck. "You can't expect me to believe that."

A little jerk of my pelvis is my pathetic attempt to unseat him. Of course it fails, and he simply bears down on me with all his weight before leaning down to whisper in my ear.

"I know how to prove your guilt, Ellen. Do you want to know how? Or do you want to confess?"

"I'm not guilty," I shiver, but it's too late for that.

A hand introduces itself into my knickers, fingers taking bold possession of their contents. My lips are split apart by inescapable probes; they pay particular attention to the swollenness of my clit and the swamp conditions that surround it.

"Oh, you need it," he confirms, his eyes bright with triumph. "You are so wet, god, and so hot and...guilty as charged, Ms. Carrington."

I shift restlessly, wanting more, inviting him to rub and push, which he does with alacrity. I am not going to argue this point.

"I'll come quietly," I moan.

"Quietly? Not if I have anything to do with it."

He's right. There is no way this insistent pressure, this sweet torment, is going to lead to anything other than the most vocal of throes. He pulls down the knickers, pushes my thighs wide and sets to work with all the energy and thoroughness his police training has imbued. His strong hands, capable fingers sliding inside me, test me for stretch and depth, finding the places that make me kick and whimper on contact.

"Open your eyes," he commands, guessing that I am close. I want to hide from his relentless scrutiny, but he will not allow it. I force them open and when I come, I watch him watching me, enjoying my surrender, relishing the confession my sex makes for me.

"Oh, good, yes," he smiles, the smile he always gives the crook at the moment of capitulation. "You've done the right thing. We'll take care of you, don't worry."

I am speechless, defeated.

"Thanks," is all I can say. Then, once his hand is out of me and he loosens his tie, "What about you?"

"What about me?"

I put it another way. "What's my sentence?"

"Your sentence?" He pulls off the tie, unbuttons his shirt with slippery-wet fingers. "Ah. I see. I'd say the punishment should fit the crime, wouldn't you?"

"Absolutely. But...look, do you mind? These cuffs are really starting to dig into me."

"Oh." The shirt is gone, the trousers next on the list. "Right. Let's..."

He pulls me up by the shoulders and rolls me over on to my

stomach. My arms are still strained but the chunky metal of the cuffs is no longer a distraction.

"So there you are." His voice is behind me, close to my ear. "Tried and found guilty. Sentenced to a good hard fuck. Bend over the dock, my dear."

Oh, he is fantastically perverse. My heart flutters with love. How does he know I have pictured this, during long dreary stints in the Crown Court?

I hear the snappity-snap of the condom, then his forearm is under my stomach, manipulating me onto my knees. The restraint of my arms forces my face down into the covers; he will have to hold on to me if he does not want me to crumple down flat at the first thrust.

Of course, he knows this—he seems to know everything— so two hands smack down onto my hips and grip me tightly, preparing me for the first taste of my shameful portion.

"The judge is watching you...everyone in the courtroom is. The stenographer is poised to record every thrust, every gasp, every little squeak that comes from your mouth. The press will have a blow-by-blow account in all the papers tomorrow, and the court sketcher is making sure he gets the curve of your ass... just...right."

I feel the tip of his cock butt my buttocks, then glide its way around the flesh, stopping for a quick poke between my cheeks before drifting down the crack to its destination.

"Did you hear what the judge said?" he whispers, guiding that fat bulb to the slick entrance awaiting it. "You're going to be made to come, at least five times a week, for a minimum of two years. No time off for good behavior. No parole. Just plenty of time spent on your back, or your knees, with a hard cock inside you. And it starts...now."

My lungs inflate and I hold the breath his sudden ingress

prompts for much longer than I should. The feeling of him, inside, filling me with his thick length, is too precious to permit me to focus on anything as mundane as exhalation. I need to take and hold this moment for as long as I can.

He eases into his rhythm, moving slowly at first, taking every opportunity to lean down and fill my ears with more of his fervid imaginings.

"See their eyes upon you. See the furious scribbling and note-taking? You're front-page news. And the collar is mine. You are my body. I caught you fair and square."

He tugs on the handcuffs, straining my shoulders, pulling me back so his cock sinks deeper. I imagine the cold sleek wood of the dock, slippery with condensation from my heat. I imagine that I am bent over, in high heels, my skirt rucked and blouse pulled open while the jury stares at my exposed nipples and creeps around the room for a better view of my ass, turning pink from the relentless pounding of my arresting officer. The sketcher captures the moment of confluence between cock and cunt, confident sweeping strokes of charcoal depicting my punishment for the edification of the masses in tomorrow's papers. He has to get my face right. He has to get that over-whelmed look into my eyes, that contortion of mouth and crum-pling of forehead, every shameful lineament of expression.

The thought of it heightens the sensation below, which is already growing with each tiny increment in Blake's pace. His dick is deadly accurate, hitting all the spots, over and over. His whisper, his thrust, his finger on my clit, his power, my surrender—all of these converge in one moment of frightening intensity, a feeling I don't immediately recognize as orgasm until the fire of it reaches my belly. I realize that I have not ripped apart at the seams. I am simply coming—coming harder than I have ever done before, and certainly not coming quietly, but coming nonetheless. What an inadequate verb it seems to describe the experience; somebody really needs to invent a better one.

But not me, and not now. Not while the cells of my brain occupy opposing ends of the universe.

I am almost surprised, on coming round, to find myself in a bedroom and not amidst the majestic trappings of Her Majesty's Crown Court. Blake has discreetly withdrawn from my well-used pussy and is lying beside me, one slightly shaky hand on my hip.

"What do you think?" he asks, his voice a little dry. He clears his throat. "Was that sentence too harsh?"

"No." I try to move my wrists. He takes the hint and uncuffs me. "Not at all. I think I got off lightly."

"Oh." He laughs tiredly. "You're not going to appeal then?"

"Not unless it's for a stiffer sentence."

I have my stiffer sentence. I have it most nights. Believe me, when the choice is available, I will always opt for the hard way.

STRAPPED

K. D. Grace

When I see him eyeing me from across the room, my stomach drops to the floor, and I wonder if he knows. Will he betray me if he does? If so, will he do it quietly, or will he make sure everyone knows what I'm up to? I contemplate leaving quietly by a side door, but before I have a chance, he sidles up to the bar next to me. I stand frozen to the spot, close enough that his arm, hard muscle beneath soft cotton, brushes mine, even though the bar isn't crowded.

My pulse is a drumroll hammering against my throat. Surely he must see it. In the mirror behind the bar I can see his sideways glances taking me in. I try not to squirm, while I take a mental inventory: jeans, loafers, tits strapped tight beneath my oversized shirt. My best friend, Alex, coached me. He says I'm good. He says my disguise is flawless. But then he never thought I'd actually go through with it, and it certainly never occurred to either of us that I might have to make a run for it wearing a strap-on.

I'm still trying to figure out what gave me away when he turns to me and nods to my barely touched beer. "What are you drinking?"

"Bud," I say, trying to wrestle my heart back into its proper spot while he orders for both of us. Then just when my nerves have nearly settled, our drinks arrive, and he turns to me and offers a half smile. "You come here often?"

Jesus, is the man actually hitting on me? Before I can respond, his face reddens and he curses under his breath. I'm taken by how young he seems. "I'm sorry. That didn't come out right. What I meant is that I've never been here before, and I'm just wondering if it's a good place. For a drink, I mean." He reddens again, lifts his beer and nearly chokes on his first gulp. Stupidly, I pound him on the back before I catch myself. I clear my throat and step back. "You all right there?" My voice is a low contralto. Sexy, I've been told, but a bit mannish. Tonight I'm counting on it.

I take a long drag from my beer and pretend to be interested in some boxing match on the muted big screen. "My first time, too," I say. "Just checking the place out."

He heaves a sigh and offers a sheepish grin that makes him seem extremely boyish, though I'd guess from the smile lines around his eyes, he's not as young as he looks. "I've never done this before." He gulps most of his beer and orders another for himself and for me.

"You're nervous," I say, wondering what I'm going to do with three Buds.

"Aren't you? I mean you seem a little, I don't know. Out of place."

He has no idea!

He leans an elbow on the bar and turns to face me. I'm struck by the long lean lines of him; not quite, but almost cowboyish beneath denim and cotton. He's not actually any taller than I am, but the illusion of height is there. His blond hair is unruly around his cheeks and down over one eye, making me want to reach out and brush it aside. His stance is open, vulnerable. His gaze rakes over my body, and I shudder in response. When his eyes meet mine, the blush crawls back up his throat, where I can see the drumroll of his own pulse, but he holds my gaze. "I've never done this before," he repeats in a half whisper. It's not exactly pleading I hear in his voice; it's something closer to curiosity and embarrassment maybe. But there's no doubt about what he wants.

I don't know what possesses me. I only came here to observe. But here I am giving him an equally hard once-over, which he endures stoically. There's no missing the beginnings of a bulge in his jeans. Then I step closer and speak next to his ear. "You want me, you do exactly as I say." Jesus, what the hell is in that beer? Whatever it is, I finish off one for courage, wipe my mouth on the back of my hand, then turn and walk out the side door into the alley with a hell of a lot more bravado than I actually feel. In my peripheral vision, I see him gulping his own courage, then he's right behind me, so close I can feel the heat of him. At the door he slips a condom and a small packet of lube into my hand, and my pussy gets twitchy and my stomach does a flip-flop.

For sure, then. This is what he wants.

Outside, I don't let him kiss me. I don't even let him touch me. Complete control is my only hope of pulling this off. I can't even allow myself to think about the utter madness of what I'm doing. I nod to his jeans. "I want to see." I'm trembling too badly to manage the technicalities of freeing his cock myself, though he's shaking pretty badly, too.

While he struggles to release himself, I stroke my strap-on

through my jeans, and he watches hungrily. My pussy buzzes like there's an electrical current passing between my legs. I never need a lot of effort to come. I can do with my brain what most chicks need a dildo for, or at least their fingers. Tonight I'm not going to need any help at all.

His balls are tucked tight up next to his slender torso in a pillow of blond curls. His heavy cock strains out toward me like a bodybuilder in full press. I step forward and shove his jeans and boxers down, then give his tight asscheeks a good feel. He grunts like I've punched him in the stomach, but as I start to kneel in front of him, he stops me. "No. I don't want that. I mean not right now. I want..." He nods to my package displayed so nicely beneath my jeans. "I want you in me." For a second I think he's going to hyperventilate, but even as he struggles to breathe, his cock surges still harder.

Barely trusting my voice, I half gasp. "Turn around then."

He does as I say. His breathing is fast and furious and his cock looks like it's about to explode. He reaches back with a hand that's none too steady and grasps one buttock, exposing his dark, tight hole, which clenches and relaxes expectantly. "Do it," he rasps, and he spreads his legs and shoves his ass back toward me.

I've never done this before. I've played with my own asshole a bit, and Alex tells me what it's like for him, but I wasn't expecting this. I spit on my fingers, saving the lube for the grand entrance. Then I carefully ease one finger inside him, and he catches a harsh breath. I fight the temptation to apologize for hurting him, but the pain must not be too bad because he thrusts and bumps back against my finger like he can't get enough.

My pussy has reached flood stage. Each time I shift and squirm against the strap-on, my clit throbs and my cunt lips feel like they're about to split the crotch right out of my jeans. I stick another finger in his ass and begin to scissor inside him. He sucks air between his teeth. "Fuck," he grunts, "Do it! Christ, just do it! I need you to do it."

In a near panic, I struggle to manage my fly and boxers with one hand, but when I need the other to maneuver my cock out, he groans. "Do it, goddamn it! I can't stand it."

"Shut up and hold still." I'm amazed at how confident I sound. "You do as I say, remember?" I'm struggling into the condom, then smearing lube, getting as much of it on my jeans as I do on my cock.

He's stroking himself fast and furious, and I'm lubing and rubbing all up and down my strap-on, shaking all over. I'm so nervous, and so damned hot, I fear I'll self-combust before I can get into him. Then, when I'm ready, I bend down and spit into his tensing gape just for good measure. I'm trembling so hard I miss on my first thrust and we both curse out loud. But the second time my aim is true. I shove in hard.

"Oh, shit!" he gasps between gritted teeth. "Fucking hell!"

"What should I do? What do you need?" I gasp, holding very still.

With a bruising hand, he reaches around, grabs my hip and pulls me so tight against him that he forces the breath out of me in a hard grunt. "I fucking need you to thrust," he growls.

And thrust I do, as hard as I can, as deep as I can. Each time I thrust, the back end of the dildo in the harness grinds against my pubic bone, causing everything between my legs to grasp and clench and swell in the slippery ride. I hold on for as long as I can, which isn't long. Neither of us manages more than a few minutes. He grunts hard, and I see him jizz the brick wall in front of us. Then I'm coming so damned hard that I'm sure there'll be broken bones.

It feels like I come for ages. It feels like I'll never stop. But when I do pull out, he's leaning against the wall gasping for breath. I yank off the condom as quickly as possible. I figure I've only got seconds to discreetly store the package before he regains his senses. Then maybe we'll go back into the bar for a quick drink. And after that... Well, what could there actually be after that? I'm not the guy he thinks I am. It took all my concentration to pull this off. Round two would no doubt be slower, more touchy-feely, more show and tell, and I can't afford to show or tell. But then I'm thinking like a woman, aren't I? Anyway, I can't risk it.

"When were you planning on telling me?" He speaks between efforts to breathe, interrupting my postcoital ruminations.

I freeze mid-tuck, realizing his back is no longer turned, and he's staring at my strap-on, the look on his face unreadable. Now I'm not only struggling with the strap-on, but I'm struggling to keep my heart from jumping out of my throat.

"Leave it," he commands, pushing my hands away and shoving my jeans down enough to get a good view of my package. Then he's not just looking, he's stroking. He releases a long breath, and I feel it low on my bare belly. "Bloody hell. It's a nice one."

"Thanks," I say. "Glad you like it."

"Why did you do it?" He seems fascinated with stroking my strap-on.

"I just wanted to know what it feels like to be a guy."

He offers a half smile. "Looks to me like it felt pretty good."

I heave a sigh of relief that he doesn't seem to be too angry. I try to resist the urge to thrust, but it's hard. The way he's stroking me—the way he's looking at me—makes me hot all over again. "Did you know all along?"

"Of course I didn't know. It's a gay bar, for fuck sake. Surely you must have known I'd want to see your cock." He gives my extension a hard tug, causing me to gasp. "It took you ages to suit up and lube. I had plenty of time for a peek." With the hand that's not stroking my cock, he takes my chin and pulls me into a deep kiss. In all the confusion buzzing through my brain, I can't keep from wondering what that expressive tongue would feel like snaking its way around my pussy.

Then it hits me: this tongue knows its way around a woman. There's no awkwardness, certainly no sense that he's not enjoying himself, and I may be a bit of a tomboy, and I may not have sex all that often, but I do know how a man feels when he's aroused.

"You're not gay," I say, when he gives me room to breathe.

For a second, he stops stroking my cock and holds my gaze. I can just make out the glint in his eyes under the muted glow of the second-story windows. "You're not the only one who can fake it."

"Why?" I ask, as his hand slides under my shirt toward my bound breasts.

"Don't get me wrong. I love women, but..." his voice drifts off as his fingers find one of the safety clasps that hold the elastic bandage in place around my tits. It's crude, I admit, but it works.

I ease my hand up to help him with the clasp, suddenly wanting him to touch me. "But you're bi-curious?"

"More than that," he gives my cock a hard stroke, and I thrust against him. I'm now working frantically at the clasps holding the bandage, and he's shoving and pushing at the binding, trying to get to my tits. "I think I might be bi. I've known for a long time that I'm attracted to men. I just never acted on it until tonight. I've never come like that before." He nods down at my cock. "I mean so hard."

The binding uncoils like a snake and falls away, parts of it draping like bunting over my cock. He moves immediately to cup and knead my small breasts, almost as though he's reassuring himself that I have all the right bits. I shove the binding off my cock and reach down to stroke his, which, amazingly, is already back at full attention and heavy against my hand. "But you knew I was a woman when I fucked you. That hardly counts as the real thing, does it?"

"Felt pretty real to me," he says. Now he turns *me* to the wall and I hear the rattle of another condom wrapper. There I am, braced against the brick, bareassed, my pussy thrust back at him like a begging mouth. There's no preamble. He's in like Flynn, and I'm in heaven, thrusting back against him, my strap-on erection bouncing merrily in front of me. He pinches my nipples and kneads me like I'm bread dough. Then he slides a hand down to stroke and jerk my silicone stiffy in rhythm with his own thrusting. Jesus, it's good! His hot breath is burning the back of my neck and I'm mewling and squirming like a wildcat, and we both come with guttural growls that rake at our throats and echo off the brick.

When it's done and we're more or less fit for decent company, I turn to face him, tucking the wadded elastic bandage into my pocket. "If you want the real thing, I think I can arrange it." We exchange cell numbers and leave without going back into the bar.

I wanted to rent a hotel room. But Alex says if our new friend, Ben—that's his name— likes fucking in the alley behind a gay bar, he's way too adventurous for that. He says to leave the venue to him.

"You've got to be kidding," I hiss in his ear as the cab drops us in front of the MaXXX Cinema in a part of town I didn't even know existed. I'm in my normal street clothes, but beneath my loose-fitting jeans, I'm packing. Alex is in his usual chinos and cotton shirt. A few men are buying tickets at the box office. They cast furtive glances toward the darkened streets before disappearing into the maw of the building between huge posters promising a triple feature XXXtravaganza. Standing there in front of one of the posters looking like he owns the place is Ben. He smiles when he sees me, and both men size each other up as I make brief introductions.

"So how are we gonna pull this off in a cinema?" I ask Alex. "Granted, no one might notice in a place like this, but I'm thinking logistics here, Alex, logistics."

"Trust me," he says, and motions us toward a door that's marked EMPLOYEES ONLY. Ben and I glance at each other, shrug, then follow. What else are we going to do?

Alex is already halfway up a dimly lit staircase by the time the door closes behind us. At the top of the stairs we follow him to another door labeled PROJECTION ROOM. Alex knocks softly and offers us a reassuring smile as we wait.

A woman with an overwhelming coif of gray hair and very large glasses opens the door, blinks magnified eyes as though the sight of us shocks her, then motions us in. The monstrosity that is the projector takes up most of the space in the cramped, dusty room. Along the tight back wall, a diminutive stepladder flanks shelves of disorderly film cans. The only furniture is a metal folding chair. The film's already rolling. Through the darkened glass that looks out onto the cinema, I catch glimpses of the opening credits flashing over a Wal-Mart Kama Sutra of thrusting and humping all done to the rhythm of what could pass as elevator music on Viagra. Beneath it all, I can just make out the metallic whir of the projector.

The woman pulls the key from her pocket and looks around

the room with a sigh. "Film's just starting," she says in a voice that sounds like it could belong to my grandmother. "Stay away from the projector, don't touch any of the films and clean up your mess. I'm not a janitor." She looks down at her watch. "You have exactly an hour, Alex. Not one second more. Then I'm coming in." She holds up the key. "No matter what perversions you lot are up to." She gives us all a disapproving glance. Then she turns her attention back to Alex. "You owe me one." She offers him a brief hint of a smile and leaves. We hear the key turn in the lock.

When we're all satisfied she's gone, Alex turns his attention to Ben. "Kitty tells me you like her as a guy." He rakes an approving gaze over him, lingering just below belt level. "But you want the real thing, don't you?" He steps forward into Ben's personal space and runs a hand over his fly, smiling at the little flinch that ends as a tight sigh in the back of Ben's throat. He takes Ben by the wrist and guides his hand to reciprocate, offering a little grunt of surprise at Ben's enthusiasm. "There, you see? This time I promise you the genuine article." He gives a nod of consent and I can see Ben's hands tremble as he opens Alex's chinos and reaches awkwardly inside.

I sit on a chair near the projector, happy to play voyeur. I watch Alex's eyelids flutter and I see the way he shifts his hips forward, one hand pushing the waistband of his chinos away. He flinches and bites his lip. Ben's a little rough on the extrication, but Alex doesn't seem to mind rough. And when the unveiling is complete, there's a collective gasp as Ben and I see my friend's large heavy cock for the first time, and I'm seriously considering taking the dildo out of the strap-on and using it on myself.

"There," Alex breathes, guiding Ben's hand along his shaft. "You like that, don't you? It feels like you, only different." He leans in and kisses Ben and nips his bottom lip with just the flick of his tongue, and I soak my panties as I shift against the chair.

But Ben's not settling for a nip. He wants the whole enchilada with all the trimmings. Still stroking and caressing Alex's cock, he pulls him close and eats at his mouth like he's starving. Alex manages to get his hand down the front of Ben's jeans and both men are thrusting against each other and I'm thrusting against myself, holding my breath, not even blinking, because I've never seen anything like this.

Alex pulls away and places a heavy hand on Ben's shoulder, and Ben totally gets it. He drops to his knees and takes Alex's cock into his mouth, nearly gagging in his overzealousness. Then Alex curls a hand in his hair and helps him find a rhythm that works for both of them.

The room is filled with slurpy, slippery sex sounds and I'm not sure some of them aren't coming from my drenched pussy rubbing against the seam of my jeans. In the flashing monochrome light of the projector, my eyes ache from watching so hard. I fumble with my jeans, pushing them down until the hard metal of the folding chair is against my ass, then I shift until I can slip some fingers between my lips. Both men glance over at me, and I realize I'm making little moaning sounds and stroking my strap-on in solidarity with the guys.

Alex pulls away with more self-discipline than I think I would have had. He helps Ben to his feet. "I showed you mine, now show me yours."

Ben nearly rips the fly out of his jeans, releasing himself, and Alex lets out a low whistle. "Kitten, I'm gonna need that chair," he calls over his shoulder.

With my jeans still down around my thighs and one hand still stroking the strap-on, I shift to the ratty-looking stepladder, and Alex takes my place on the chair, pulling Ben by the belt loop to stand in front of him. He sucks and strokes and admires until Ben is practically thrusting in his face, then Alex pulls away. "Now that I've paid my respects to your cock, turn around and let me see your ass."

The lighting's poor, and with the flash from the projector and all, maybe I only imagine that the color has gone from Ben's face. Maybe I'm only speculating that he might be feeling just a little frisson of fear about now. After all, Alex has a big cock. Ben's lips are a tight, straight line pressed against his teeth as he slowly turns to offer his tender pink ass. Alex gets right to it. He buries his face between the pillows of Ben's buttcheeks and his tongue goes dancing around that luscious little pucker. Ben nearly goes through the ceiling with that first contact. Alex's tongue is long, and I'm almost certain it's prehensile, and Ben's cock is jerking and throbbing like it's alive. I can't tell by the look on his face if he's in ecstasy or agony. I'm pretty sure it's the former as Alex reaches around to cup his balls and knead them like they're his favorite new toy.

"Oh, god," Ben gasps. "I can't stand it."

Alex clamps down on his cock with his thumb just under the head. "Hold it. This is no quickie you're having here. We've got a whole hour."

Ben's eyes are clenched shut and he's sucking hard at his lower lip, trying to regain control.

But I don't have to keep control. I come like it's Christmas, knowing full well I can do it again as often as I want, and after all, we do have a whole hour.

Before I can get too smug Alex calls to me. "Saddle up, Kitten. I want to see if you're as good as Ben here thinks you are." He stands up. Without skipping a beat, his fingers replace his tongue in the anal tango.

Ben watches, round-eyed, as I slip into a condom and lube up. Then I thrust my mock cock into Alex's asshole like I know what I'm doing. The thought that I'm pegging my best friend in what has been up until now a no-go zone already has me riding the edge of another orgasm. And watching him lube up and press his condomed cock up against Ben's tight asshole, the same asshole I was buried to the hilt in only three nights ago, is enough to send me over. I gasp and falter, but manage to regain my balance as Alex thrusts in and I hear Ben suck oxygen and grunt hard.

"Oh, fuck!" he gasps. "Jesus, I've never felt anything like..." Then he's holding on for dear life, one hand on his cock, the other braced against his knee to support the combined weight of both of us bumping and humping behind him. I can feel Alex clenching and thrusting back against me, then he grunts in between efforts to breath, "Kitten, I'm gonna have to ask you to disengage."

I do as he says and he plops down on the chair, both arms wrapped around Ben's waist, dragging him down onto his lap still fully impaled. Then he kisses Ben on the neck and reaches around to cup his balls. "You can come on the floor if you want," he says next to Ben's ear. "But then you'll have to clean it up unless you want Betty to skin you alive. Or you can finish off sweet in Kitty's hot cunt. Bet I know which you'll choose." He nips his earlobe.

Ben catches my eye and nods. And quick as a wink, I suit up his cock, pausing just long enough to take off my shirt so he can get to my tits. Then I simply turn around, ease back onto his lap and let him push in.

There's a wild layer-cake of thrusting, and I'm feeling it all the way to the crown of my head by the time the guys are getting close. I'm no longer even sure what planet I'm on. The chick in the porn film is caterwauling louder and louder for the guy pumping her to fuck her harder. The lights flash around us. But it's all just white noise to our own chorus of wet grunts and moans. The room is awash in the humid scent of sweaty males rutting and the wicked hot smell of my cunt spasming almost continually.

Ben comes first, and being sandwiched in the middle, he nearly upsets the chair. He catches me just before I'm launched across the room into the film cans, and just as Alex explodes beneath us all.

We just manage to get tidied and tucked and make sure all the telltale evidence of a good time is cleared away before the lock turns in the door and Betty's back. She waves us all out and turns her attention to threading the next film of the triple feature into the projector.

We file out into the night and pile into Ben's Jeep. We grab sustenance at a McDonald's drive-thru. The night's still young and we'll need all the energy we can get. Alex has a friend who manages an all-night liquor store not far from his neighborhood. There's a great storeroom at the back, he informs us, lots of kegs and crates and tarps and even a dolly or two. The place has real potential, he says, eyeballing both of us like he's still hungry, and we're next on the menu. The friend owes him a favor, he says. We all agree it's time he pays up.

I grab the roll bar as Ben downshifts through the changing traffic light, and we're in—all of us. In like Flynn.

BENEATH
MY SKIN

Shanna Germain

I'm afraid."

The words coming from my lips are barely audible. My face is pushed into the sheets. My chest is, too, so that only my ass is in the air before him, raised and blooming with red handprints. Kade's handprints. No one else touches my ass. This is the deal we have.

"You should be." His voice is gravelly and deep, but not mean. Never mean. Even as he speaks the words that make my stomach feel cold, the rest of me is hot. My face prickles with a nervous, excited blush, even though it's mostly hidden by my tangled hair. My palms sweat their heat into the sheets. Even the little folds behind my bent knees are growing slippery. And the space between my thighs—which he's teasing with one finger, soft strokes that belie his eventual plan—that space is the hottest of all, opening around his cool fingertip, liquid and lava.

His other hand circles the curves of my still-warm ass. The skin pulses beneath his touch, each passing stroke over the tender skin pulling my breath back into my mouth. I push my face harder into the sheets, biting at the fabric to muffle my gasps.

"No," he says, and he stops touching. Just like that. I know why—he likes to hear me, likes to listen to the groans and moans and the cries that erupt from my mouth when he pleases or teases me.

I let go of the sheet, feel my teeth drag along the material. As soon as my mouth opens, he cups his hand back on one side of my ass, digs his nails into the pinkened curve. The sound that I tried to hold back before rises now, sliding through my throat, a mix of embarrassment and want that makes me wince.

"Good slut," he says. "Much, much better."

I can't help but shiver at his words—the way he calls me his slut, the way the sound of it makes his voice lower to a near growl—it still makes me ache inside, so much that I want something, anything, buried in me.

Instead of filling me like I want, Kade's hands move away from my ass, leaving me feeling unprotected somehow, exposed to the view and the air and whatever might come next. Which, with Kade, might be anything.

This time, it's a question. Actually, it's a question in the form of a command.

"Now," he says. "Tell me why you're scared."

Behind me, before I can answer, I hear the click of the knife opening in his hands. *Click,* closed. *Click,* open again. The very sound makes my breath speed up, matching the beat of my pulse. Even with my eyes closed, I know what he looks like behind me: on his knees, one hand lowering to brush the roundness of my ass, the other swinging in that small, habitual gesture he has, the small black knife opening and closing with his movements.

I'm so caught up in the image of him that I forget his question, and I don't even notice when the sound of the knife stops.

Then the edge of it—the wide part of the blade, I can tell by feel—is sliding along the side of my back, following the muscles downward. His voice is soft. His blade is not. But it doesn't cut. It never cuts. This is just a reminder of power, of control, and I hold my body so still that I barely breathe. He doesn't have to tie me, although he could and he has before. He knows that I am well trained, that I will remain still for him just because he says so.

"Why"—he says, each word coming slowly, each syllable met with another downstroke of the back of the knife—"are you scared?"

I know the answer, don't I? I should. This, I know, is important. But all I can do is think about the knife that's dragging along my skin. It's so safe like this, the blunt edge, the way he threads it carefully around my muscles and skin, and yet it opens me up like the slut that I am, makes me want to beg him to fuck me. So why do I want more if it scares me so much? Is it because it scares me so much?

"I don't know."

"Mm-hm," he says. "You don't know."

And he shifts back on the bed. I can hear him pull away, but I don't open my eyes. The sound that comes out of me is instinctual, a rising whine of want and need that would embarrass me if I weren't already embarrassed, if my ass weren't already in the air, my head down, my need so evident in the arc of my body, the tremble of my hips and thighs.

The knife clicks again. A finger returns to my pussy, teases along the very point of my clit and seconds later is replaced by something else. Something harder, the edges scraping against my soft, wet skin so that I gasp. His voice drops to the whisper that always reassures me, the sound of safety as it slides against my ear and softly caresses that flight-and-fight response in my brain. "It's just the handle. Closed. See?" I can't see, not with my eyes closed, not with Kade and the knife behind me, not with the dark specks that are popping in my brain, but my body unclenches at his words. The handle teases the length of my pussy, slow hard strokes until I know I am wetting the knife, darkening the already dark handle. My ass and hips meet his strokes, arching back, asking for more, more, harder.

He pretends he doesn't hear, pulls the knife away, a constant tease, and I am left wiggling my hips in a useless gesture of want.

"Open your eyes," he says. I do, and he's crouched beside the bed, his golden-brown eyes staring into mine. Slowly, slowly, he raises the knife until it's in my view—black handle, silver blade, small enough to fit easily into his palm, the blade long and sharp enough to make my stomach clench. It's open now. Was it before? I don't know. I have to trust him, don't I? Believe what he says.

He turns it so that I can see more of the handle, where it's shined with my juices. With a single movement, he licks me from the tool. Slow, purposeful, so that I can see him do it, can see how the taste of me pulls his eyes to a darker gold.

When he's done, he sets the knife, still open, on the bed. It lies against the blood-red sheets like a warning, like a tease. His nails softly etch the side of my face as he stands to leave.

"You think about it," he says. "And when you decide you want it, you let me know."

There is nothing I hate more than being by myself, holding my position, thinking about things. I like movement, I like the rush, I like the adrenaline and fear and pleasure that forces the thoughts away. Kade knows this. It is why he does both things—why he gives me the things I want, and also why he forces me not to have them.

I breathe deep and stare down at the knife. It looks so much less menacing, so much less arousing, when it isn't in his hands. Against the sheets, it's shiny and sharp but it's also soulless, inanimate. Almost safe. It's when Kade picks it up, opens it up, curls his fingers around the dark handle: that's when it becomes the object of my desire, the thing that sends my blood running and my clit thumping.

There is no punishment if I get up without asking for the knife.

There is no punishment if I ask for the knife.

There is only punishment if I do not do as he asked: if I do not stay here, hold my position, think about what he's given to me.

So I stay there, on my hands and knees, ass up, head down, and I look at the knife for a long time.

We've been working up to this for weeks. In so many ways, it's been like planning for a wedding. Not that he and I would ever get married. We are in what we call a sinship. It's like a relationship only without the bad parts. I guess that's what happens when you're both in your late thirties and each have one good-gone-bad marriage behind you. Live separate, sin together. It's kind of our motto.

Kade started it by taking me to the knife store. The way and why of how I love knives is hard to explain, but I made the mistake of telling him about it, and he latched on the way he does. It's part of why he turns me on so much—he pays attention to my every little lust, spoken in passing, and then he puts it in action. It's also why he scares me so much.

"Which one do you like?" Kade had asked, gesturing to the rows and rows of knives beneath the glass. They were all gorgeous, so many colors and styles that I could only shake my head. The man behind the counter, big shouldered, dark eyed, was looking at me with a wolfish grin, an "I know why you're here" grin that made my cheeks hard and hot. I ducked my head, letting my hair fall over my face.

In response, he fisted his hand in my hair, pulled my head back so that I was looking at both the knives and at the knife-seller, whose grin grew wider, sharper as he watched me. "Fine prey," he said, never taking his gaze off me, a fat tongue sliding out to coat his top lip. "Fine prey like that deserves a quality knife."

"Agreed," Kade said. And suddenly there was this electricity in the room, between the two of them: two hunters in the same territory, sharpening their desires against each other. I was nothing more than a rabbit to them, going so still that I thought I could make myself invisible.

Then Kade twisted the already-caught hair harder in his grip, let his fingers rake and pull through my strands while he pushed the front of my hips hard against the glass counter, not talking to me at all. "So, let's find something that the pretty prey likes, shall we? Since she's the one whose skin it's going to be against."

Fuck. I nearly came like that, against the counter, in front of this strange man and anyone who might have walked in the door. Kade's hip pushed against me, sliding so I could feel just the tip of his cock tucked into his jeans, the already-hardening length beneath the fabric. He held me like that, pinned between the cold glass counter and the heat of his hips, reaching around me to pick up the knives from the counter, flicking them open and closed in front of me. The ones he really liked, he would draw the back of the blade along the inside of my arm, laughing when goose bumps broke out. On the other side of the counter, the knife-seller stood with his arms crossed unless he was handing Kade a knife, looking at ease, only his still smile and the growing outline of his cock in his black pants showing his pleasure at the scene.

Kade had two knives on the counter—a blood-red one with a

partly serrated blade and a black one with a thin, sharp-looking blade that reflected my flushed face when he held it up. Kade has a thing for red, especially blood-red, and I thought for sure he'd choose that. I hoped so—it looked less menacing, less sharp, almost as though it was just a toy and not dangerous at all.

"Black or red?" he asked me, watching my face.

I opened my mouth to answer, but he was already turning away. "Good choice. Black it is. We'll take it."

"And no bag necessary. I'll be using it before we get home."

Surprisingly, the first thing Kade did when he got in the car was to take the knife out of its box and hand it over to me. It weighed more than I expected, fitting into my palm and hanging off it like a live thing. "Get familiar with it," he said. "Open and close it. The blade is seriously sharp though. I wouldn't recommend touching the edge."

"But..." I was confused, and disappointed. I didn't want to learn about it. I didn't want to hold it or use it. I wanted *him* to wield it, to scare me and arouse me with it.

He turned from the wheel, his expression saying everything. Those golden eyes could turn into steel if I disobeyed, especially when it was something important. "Handle it," he said. "Or I'll return it right now."

I handled it. The whole ride home, as he took the side streets and went slow, I fondled the gift he'd given me. At first, I was afraid to open it, so I held it, letting the weight of it rest on my palm. With my other hand, I traced the lines of the handle, the almost filigree-like design in it. It could have been a flower. Or snakes entwined.

Finally, I opened it. Not like Kade did. A slow, soft open that made my pulse stutter in my wrist. He wasn't kidding—the blade was so sharp and thin. I could see how sharp it would be against someone's skin, how easily it could cut right through body and bone. It made me want to throw it away, just roll down my window and chuck it into the road. I was afraid to admit that it also made me wet. I could feel the heat soaking my jeans, even before Kade reached over and put his free hand between my legs, curling his fingers into damp fabric.

Still, he was right. Handling it made me more afraid. But it also made me less afraid. And, beneath that, the other thing that I knew was true, even if I wasn't sure I wanted to admit it yet: afraid or not, I wanted it. I wanted that knife in Kade's hands. I wanted him to cut my clothes off, piece by piece, the knife so close to my skin, but not touching. I wanted him to bend me over and fuck me with it. But more than that, I wanted to know what it felt like when he put that blade against my skin, scraped it over my back, dragged the tip between my shoulder blades. I wanted to hold so still that I was sweating, to hear his voice above me, reassuring me while he fingered me with one hand and cut me open with the other.

On the bed now, I take a deep breath and remind myself this is what I wanted, what I asked for: To be more naked than naked, to shed my skin, literally. To be bared to his hands and eyes, to be exposed by his skill and blade. I remind myself that I can trust him—he pushes me to the edge, but never farther. He knows what he's doing.

I dip my head down then, taste the metal of the blade as I catch it carefully between my teeth to pick it up. The feel of it in my mouth is so intimate that I groan softly around the blade.

When he comes back, he'll find me. He'll know I am ready.

The knife is heavier than I thought, and he doesn't come back for a long time. I hold it tight between my teeth and lips, trying to breathe around it. Trying not to cut myself in the process. Now that I'm used to it, my body has dried up, sweat and juices, and I can't remember if I'm aroused or just holding this object out of rote and ritual. I'm considering dropping it, but then he'd think I don't want him to use it.

Finally, I hear his footsteps. My teeth ache. My lips are so dry I swear I can feel them cracking. The knife has been in my mouth for a long time now. It's become part of me. I know its edges and its flavor. I am still afraid, but not the way I was before. That was the kind of fear that would have made me jump and clench, that could have put me in danger. This fear is sharply honed, as finely pointed as the blade in my mouth, and it narrows into a straight line at my clit.

"Open," he says, and I drop the knife from my mouth into his hand.

He catches it easily, flicks it open where I can see the blade shine. "Good slut."

Instantly, I'm wet again. All that time waiting slips away and my body returns to where it was, hips rising up into the air in want. I lick the bit of dryness from my lips, my tongue already salivating around the missing taste of metal.

Kade presses me down with the flat of his palm, until I am a long straight line on the bed. One hand reaches between my thighs, a few fingertips stroking.

"Still scared?" he asks.

"Yes. No."

"Perfect." The not-sharp edge of the blade makes a few slow, long sweeps across my back. I hold myself still, don't arch up into his touch, even though that's what I want. Harder. Stronger. Faster.

He sees the restrained movement. "Do I need to tie you?"

"No."

"Good. Breathe."

I exhale, then exhale some more, pushing out all the breath I have in me, emptying my lungs and then whatever reserve lies beneath my lungs. And then I am still, not just the outside, but the inside, in that place that never, ever quiets.

Kade turns the knife, lets the very tip drag across my skin. The pain is not as bad as I expected, a sharpness like a nail. It is both dulled and heightened by his slippery fingers slowly teasing my clit. It's a very light touch. He's breaking my skin, but barely. Like the scrape of a fingernail. Not even a paper cut.

The next path is spine to shoulder, a sweeping drag of blade. He isn't cutting into me, I don't think, not enough to draw blood, but it's hard to tell.

I breathe with my whole body.

He draws with his whole blade.

Together, Kade and the knife create their unknowable pattern across my skin. Every touch of the blade sends me somewhere deeper and somewhere higher. My nipples are hard and sensitive, and when I exhale, they brush against the sheets in a sharp ache that's so different from the thin lines of pain across my shoulders.

Each pull of the knife is different from the last, and the same, too. The way it starts, sharp pinprick; the way it slides, slippery line of pain; the way it ends, fading so quick into nothing that I am already aching for the next one. I feel like a knife myself, lying so straight and still, everything honed. Invincible even as Kade is opening my skin, exposing the part of me that no one else has ever seen.

"Don't come," he says. "You'll shake too much." His voice is low and growled, his breath tight and quick, and I realize suddenly how much restraint he is showing, how hard he must be working to hold back.

This alone makes me want to come. I let out a sound that might be a response, or it might just be the final bit of breath leaving me.

"No, please," I say, which makes no sense, but my mouth is not working, my brain is not connecting to my tongue. "I can't..."

"Just a few more," Kade says.

I breathe.

He stops drawing.

"Done," he says.

At the same time, he sends his fingers deep inside me and leans down to lick the edges of his work. The heat of his mouth, the slow draw of his tongue over my teased skin, his fingers curling inside me while his thumb circles my clit—it sends me down and up, every bit of me clenching and releasing until my head goes dark. I see red and black, I feel red and black—they're the colors of my nipples against the sheets, his fingertip across my pulsing clit, his hand holding the knife against my back.

When my head stops spinning and sliding, Kade kisses my neck, softly. "Beautiful," he whispers. "You have to see."

I reach for him instead, my hands trying to find his body. Right now, all I want is his cock—I want to see his arousal from what he's doing, to wrap my tongue around the curve of his head while my back pulses and aches, to lie down on the sheets, feeling them scratch my tender shoulders with every thrust inside me.

"Later," he says.

He holds me tight, then helps me up and positions me so that my length is in the bedroom mirror, my back to the mirror. One of Kade's hands is on my neck, the other still holds the blade.

I turn my head so I can see. Kade's blade has cut me, not to bleeding, but to marking. A pair of raspberry-colored wings feathers out across my back and shoulders.

"It's…" I don't have any words for what I feel when I see it.

I am marked. Seen. Exposed. I am all of these things, but only for Kade. Only because he makes me do the things that I am most afraid of, the things I want most of all. I feel a sense of relief, as though I've passed a test, a test of strength and arousal, of my ability to be stretched and broken open.

"Thank you," I say, and I sag against his body, let him hold me up.

"I'm not done," he says, and his voice shifts, deepens. His hand on my neck tightens, and fear slides down through my belly, clinches my pussy in a tight pulse. The knife in his hand flashes and shines. "In fact, I've hardly begun."

"On your knees, slut," he says and when I don't move fast enough, he bends me down on the bed, his nails digging at the back of my neck as he forces me into position. I shiver against him, let out a noise. I can't help it.

"Aw," he tsks. "Are you afraid, slut?" he wants to know, his teeth edging my ear, that hard edge cutting the corners of his voice.

"Yes," I say. My voice is muffled by the sheets, by the greedy clenches of my pussy, by the pulse that pounds in my throat.

The point of the knife draws lazy circles across my back, begins a soft, slow cut into my skin just as he slides the tip of his cock between my legs.

"Good," he says. "You should be."

COMFORT
FOOD

Donna George Storey

One bite of that butterscotch pudding and suddenly I knew everything was going to be all right.

If one of my more sensible friends had been sitting at the table with me, she would have told me the pudding had nothing to do with it. The new buoyant sensation in my chest was the natural outcome of a relaxed vacation by myself at a charming country inn. The crazy grin on my face, the almost sexual quickening of my breath, were but a long-delayed visceral understanding of all the work I'd done in therapy over the last year. There was no need to wallow in misery any longer. Dylan's affair and my subsequent decision to divorce him were only symptoms of our buried grief for the real death of our marriage years before. It was time to move on.

However, since I was alone and had no need to be reasonable, I knew the epiphany was all in the pudding. Perhaps it was the creamy smoothness caressing my tongue like satin? Or the bottomless depth of flavor: caramel, tropical vanilla and an almost floral sweet cream, all mixed together with something else mysterious, alluring, even addictive?

Whatever the reason for the magic, at that moment, I was very glad to be alive.

When I finished my dessert, resisting the urge to lick the bowl clean, I waved over the pretty waitress.

"Does your chef give out recipes? I'd love to make this pudding at home to remember my vacation."

"Actually, I'm new here, I'm not sure," she said, blushing. "I'll ask Joseph."

I gazed out the window overlooking the lodge's perennial garden, wondering what trials of the spirit awaited that fresh, young thing in her life ahead. Or would she be one of the fortunate few who enjoyed the thrill of love without tasting its sorrows? Did such a person even exist?

I was still lost in my reverie when I became aware of a stocky male form in a white chef's coat standing beside my chair. Already my nerves were singing from the warmth of his body, his scent of cumin and olive oil, but when I looked up and met his sky-blue eyes, my pulse skipped two beats. "Joseph" was younger than I expected.

"I'm glad you enjoyed your dessert," he said.

"The pudding was exquisite," I said, pleased at the strangely sultry depth of my voice. "I'd love to have the recipe as a souvenir of my stay here."

The boy chef hesitated. I took advantage of the pause to drink in his smooth skin kissed with a touch of five o'clock shadow, the sensual yet determined mouth. Beneath his chef's toque, his chestnut hair was tousled and very touchable. And who wouldn't be enchanted by those cerulean eyes, boring into my soft, secret places more pleasurably than my favorite ice-blue dildo?

Here was a tasty dish indeed.

Finally he spoke. "Again, I'm delighted you liked it, but I'm afraid I don't give out my recipes."

I'm not quite sure what possessed me then. I'd spent most of the last year either sobbing or staring off into space in a self-pitying gloom, but suddenly a fire I'd thought dead forever sparked to life.

I tilted my head and smiled. "You remind me of my great-aunt Patricia. She was a fabulous cook, and I know she seduced more men with her culinary talents than many a beauty queen. But, tragically, she refused to share her recipes. They all died with her. Isn't it a shame to deprive the world of your treasures?"

Joseph folded his arms. "I'm planning on being around for a while."

"It might be a lonely existence. Pleasure was meant for sharing."

"That's the price I have to pay," he replied saucily. "But I will tell you one thing. When you make pudding, never use ultra-pasteurized cream. The processing kills the flavor. Just plain pasteurized is what you're looking for. Start with quality ingredients and you can't go wrong."

I shrugged. None of this was news to me. "Thanks for the tip."

"My pleasure." He emphasized the last word ever so slightly. "You have a great evening now, ma'am."

"Hey, wait," I called after him. "At least tell me what kind of vanilla beans you use."

He paused, midstep.

"They're Tahitian, aren't they?" I continued. "There's no mistaking those floral notes."

Joseph wheeled around, his eyes glowing with new respect.

"You're right," he said, "I do use Tahitian vanilla beans."

"That didn't hurt, did it? Now I'd guess you use brown sugar, but the flavor's so rich, it could be caramelized white."

He smiled. "Sorry, no comment. I'm onto your tricks, ma'am."

"You haven't seen anything yet." I met his gaze. He *was* a luscious young fellow. "Maybe you'd better get back to your kitchen before you divulge any more professional secrets."

Pudding aside, it had been a long time since I'd enjoyed anything as much as making that boy blush.

That night, in my bungalow tucked away at the far corner of the mountain resort, I finally convinced the baby-faced chef to spill all.

It was perhaps too easy in the end. Boys that age will do anything to get their rocks off, and at forty-four I knew all the ways to bring young men to their knees.

But that was dessert.

First came the appetizer: peeling off his sauce-streaked chef coat, and the Coldplay T-shirt he wore underneath.

"Give me the recipe for that pudding," I demanded as I ran my hands over his broad chest and shoulders.

"My apologies, ma'am, but there's nothing you can do to make that happen." His words rang with conviction, but his eyes fluttered closed.

"Oh, no?" I raked my fingertips over his biceps, circled my way down over the sensitive skin of his arm to his wrist.

He sighed.

I grasped his large, sturdy hand, the one that chopped and stirred and coddled ingredients into wondrous, life-changing elixirs, and brought it to my lips. Taking his index finger in my mouth, I slowly sucked it down, like a cock. He whimpered and shifted his weight. I let his finger float in the soft, liquid heat of my mouth for a moment before I used my tongue on him—flicks and swirls and lapping strokes, a little preview of the things I intended to do to another long, stiff part of his anatomy.

"There's more of that if you tell me the recipe."

"No...I can't...I..."

Smiling mischievously, I took his fuck-you finger in my mouth, fellating it with all my skill until I swear it stiffened and quivered in release. All the while, he was mewing and purring, making sweet feline sounds of pure submission.

My blood was roused and I pulled off, licking the drool from my lips. "You like that, don't you? But what you really want is for me to do the same thing to your cock."

"Yes." His voice was hoarse with need.

I knelt before him. His cock was so hard, the fly was practically splitting open from the throbbing pressure. I unbuckled his belt, then yanked down his trousers and briefs. My eyes narrowed in hunger at the vision of that ruddy sausage rearing up between his thighs.

"What a delicious hunk of meat. God, I want to suck it."

"Please," he whispered. "Your mouth is so hot and wet. When you licked my fingers, I thought I was going to come in my pants."

"But you'd rather come in my mouth?"

This time his "Yes," was a low, beseeching moan.

"You know what you have to do first," I taunted him.

I saw a single tear of frustration roll down his cheek. "I'm sorry, I can't tell you. It was my grandmother's special dessert. I promised her on her deathbed I'd never give it to a stranger."

"Don't you think we'll be pretty intimate if your dick is buried in my throat? Even Granny would have to agree." I wrapped my hand around his cock and pumped slowly. The shaft thickened and swelled, and the head was so red and weepy, it threatened to burst like a ripe fruit.

"All you have to do is give me that recipe and you'll get the blow job of a lifetime," I cooed.

Now his legs were shaking and he was panting like an animal. "Oh, fuck, all right. Suck it and I'll tell you. Just suck it, please."

I touched the flat of my tongue to the sensitive spot beneath the head. His whole body shivered.

"For eight servings, you start with a cup of brown sugar..." The words caught in his throat.

"Don't hold anything back now," I warned him, unzipping my own jeans and jamming one hand down between my legs.

"Okay, it's *dark* brown sugar...oh, god, keep licking it, please."

I gave him one long wet swipe of my tongue from shaft to head.

"Mix in five tablespoons of cornstarch..."

I closed my lips around the helmet of his glans.

"Press the cornstarch into the sugar with the back of a wooden spoon..." He swallowed the words in a groan as I sucked his stocky shaft all the way inside.

Shifting the hand I've wedged into my jeans into the proper position, I started to strum my clit. I was so hot and swollen down there, I knew it wouldn't be long.

"Slowly stir in two cups of milk and two cups of heavy cream, not the ultrapasteurized kind though, and...oh, fuck, oh." He thrust his hips and pawed my hair as he shot his own dish of sweet cream pudding into my mouth.

This was the image that finally pushed me over the edge as I fingered myself on my bed, my body wracked by a series of spasms that made me thrash so wildly, the mattress creaked in protest.

It had been a hell of a long time since I'd come so hard.

I laughed softly as I stretched my shaky limbs like a cat. I was soaked in sweat, and my palate tasted faintly of semen, although I couldn't even remember the last time I'd given Dylan a blow job. For so long, sex for me had mostly been with my hand, give or take a few mechanical rebound fucks with Dylan's old friend from his college days who "always had a thing for me." Just to prove I could still do it.

I was surprised at how much I missed the sensation of cock in my mouth.

That boy chef had served me up another very sweet surprise this evening. I wondered if I'd ever get the chance to thank him properly.

When I opened my eyes the next morning, I half expected to see Joseph's face on the pillow beside me. No such luck, but I did find myself with a new and very welcome companion: a burst of desire to *do* something.

After a quick breakfast—a peek through the kitchen door revealed the morning cook was not Joseph—I decided to use my last day of vacation to take advantage of the "twenty miles of beautiful hiking trails" around the resort.

With a sunny August sky cut by a cooling breeze, the weather was so perfect I could have ordered it off a menu. Thanks to the pudding and the fantasy blow job, all of my senses were heightened. I reveled in the shape of each leaf growing along the path, the sound of the birdsong, the clean scent of baked earth and oxygen-rich air. And of course, all the time I was thinking of Joseph. What was he doing now? What experience in his brief life made him wary of sharing his recipes? He was a cook who clearly enjoyed eating. Would his cock be as solid and sturdy as the rest of his body? And most intriguing of all—could his semen really taste like vanilla cream pudding?

Thirty years ago, I would have called these obsessive musings a crush, but I was wise enough now to know it had nothing to do with Joseph himself. It was all about me. I was a woman who could feel and want and enjoy life's sensual pleasures. My desire made me more interesting to myself.

I must have been walking for over an hour in a daze of lust when I wandered into a clearing to find the very object of my dreams standing before me. For a moment I thought I was hallucinating, but a few blinks reassured me that it was in fact the real Joseph, looking especially fetching in his off-duty jeans.

When he saw me, he seemed equally flustered.

"How did you find this place?" If I didn't know better, I'd say the boy was afraid.

I noticed then that the large metal bucket at his feet was half full of dark berries. We were standing in a wild blackberry grove, which Joseph, with his secretive nature, probably hoped to keep to himself.

The image of myself as a culinary predator amused me, and I laughed. "Don't worry, I'm not stalking you to get that recipe. I was just trying to work up an appetite for dinner. Are we having blackberry cobbler tonight?"

Joseph laughed, too, and returned to his work, his lusciously large fingers closing around the fattest, darkest berries with impressive speed. "There won't be enough for a cobbler this late in the season. I'll probably do a blackberry sauce for the rice pudding."

"Oooh, rice pudding? You can have your fancy, flourless chocolate torte any day, give me a good dish of homey rice pudding, and I'm in heaven." I hadn't meant to sound so much like a gushing teenager, but I was telling him the truth.

"You like comfort food, then?" he said, his expression warming noticeably.

"I suppose I do. And you like to make it?"

"Very much. It's not as glamorous as fusion or the Chez Panisse rip-offs, but I think there's a lot of potential in home-style cooking. Actually I'm talking with some investors now about opening my own place in the city. Diner food, but raised to a new level."

"That sounds wonderful," I said. "I'm sure it will be a great success. Everyone needs comfort, right?"

"I hope so." He smiled at me for just a little too long, then turned back to his berries.

The silence between us pressed down on my flesh like a warm hand. I was so hot for this sweet young thing, I could barely breathe. I was thinking up a way to make a graceful exit before I actually pounced on him right there, when Joseph spoke again.

"Are you in the food business? You seem to know your ingredients."

"Me? No, it's just a hobby. Although I haven't cooked much since my divorce," I blurted out, then blushed. As if the boy would even care if an old bag like me were attached or not.

"Well, I was impressed," he said. "Do you mind doing me a favor...I'm sorry, I didn't catch your name?"

"Natalie...Natalie Weston. And you are?"

"Joseph Sokolsky," he nodded politely. His mother had certainly raised him right. "So, Natalie, would you mind tasting a few of these berries?"

"Sure." I plucked two berries from his outstretched hand. My fingers brushed his palm, sending a jolt of lust straight to my pussy. I forced myself to breathe slowly. "What am I looking for?"

"Just taste it," he said, his eyes fixed on my face.

I popped the fruit in my mouth and chewed. My eyes shot open in surprise. "Oh."

"What?" Joseph leaned toward me.

"They're fabulous. I don't think I've ever had blackberries so sweet. I can taste the slow sunshine in them, the work of nature's patient hand. You could never get something like this in a store."

"I couldn't have said it better myself." His smile was sunshine in itself. "Well, I'll definitely be using these in a sauce tonight then. If you like it, I'm sure the less discerning guests will eat it up."

I blushed again, dizzy from the compliment. Funny how I was worried about the difference in our ages, when at that instant, I felt all of fourteen.

The hike left me famished, and I decided to have an early dinner. Not to mention I figured I'd have a better chance for one last chat with Joseph before the crowds descended.

I sauntered past the hostess's podium and peeked into the open door of the kitchen. Two sous chefs were busy at the stove, and the waitress was dropping lemon slices into pitchers of ice water. Just then Joseph himself appeared beside the young woman with a spoon in his hand.

"I need a guinea pig, Jackie. It's the sauce for the pudding."

He eased the spoon into her mouth like a mama bird feeding her baby.

"'S good," she murmured, her mouth still full.

He clucked his tongue. "All you're gonna give me is 'good?'"

She giggled. "No, I mean great. Everything you make is wonderful."

Joseph punched her lightly on the arm. "That's why you're

my favorite waitress. Hey, it's almost five-thirty. You'd better get your pretty self out there to hand the hungry lions their chow."

"Lions?" "Chow?" The insults snapped me out of my voyeur's trance and I made a quick retreat to the lobby. I was blushing again, but with a new emotion: unadulterated shame. How ridiculous I was to imagine a boy like him might actually think I was special. Joseph was quite simply a ladies' man. Females were just toys to bat around in his big, clever paws. The young pussies were for teasing and fucking—he'd have that girl in bed before the end of the week, no doubt. Flirting with me was just a passing amusement, just to show he could charm us all.

My first impulse was to slink back to my room. However, my stomach was growling so badly, I decided to take a short walk around the grounds, then come back when I could blend into the surroundings.

Unfortunately, the dining room was full when I got back. Jackie seated me at a table near the kitchen, where I caught frequent, and now unwelcome, glimpses of Joseph at work through the swinging door. It was childish of me, but I bypassed the chef's recommended specials—risotto cake with prawns and pistachio pesto, summer vegetable galette with green beans à la Nicoise—and went for the pedestrian salad with roasted beets and goat cheese.

I forced down the greens with little enjoyment, then asked for the check. To my surprise, Jackie slipped a large plate in front of me instead.

"Compliments of the chef," she murmured.

I stared down at the plate, which immediately brought to mind a modern painting. The composition was artful indeed: a small molded rice pudding crowned with two whole blackberries, floating in a crisscross net of glistening indigo sauce.

Under any other circumstances, I would have been salivating

in delight, but now I just wanted to cry. "I'm sorry, but I'm not feeling well. I don't think I can eat this."

She whisked the plate away, but soon returned with a carefully folded paper bag. "Joseph asked me to wrap it up for you in case you're feeling better later."

I instinctively glanced toward the kitchen. The door opened just a crack to reveal Joseph's frowning face gazing out at me.

I bit back a smile.

Apparently, I had the power to hurt him, too.

As soon as I got back to my room, I tore open the bag and ripped into the paper box inside. The waitress—or Joseph—had thoughtfully included a napkin and a plastic spoon, but like some wild beast, I pinched off a chunk of the rice pudding with my fingers and jammed it into my mouth.

The moan that escaped from my lips made me glad I'd retreated to my private lair. It was, quite simply, the most delicious rice pudding I'd ever eaten in my life. The texture was mousse-like, rich with cream but airy as a cloud. I tasted a kiss of rum, a heartier vanilla than the day before. Mexican perhaps? I'd only gotten a mere ribbon of sauce in my first mouthful, but it did indeed taste like the essence of summer sunshine.

Joseph might be a recipe hoarder and an incorrigible flirt, but when it came to pudding, the guy was a fucking genius.

Hurt pride and misdirected lust were mere distractions in the face of such greatness. I knew then what I had to do. But first I savored the pudding slowly, smacking my lips, purring my approval, scooping up the remnants of sauce from the box with my fingers and sucking them clean.

It was near ten o'clock when I walked boldly into the kitchen and asked for the chef. The remaining assistant pointed me to a small room in the back corner.

Joseph looked older sitting at a desk covered with papers and charts, his brow creased with concern.

"Sorry to disturb you," I said, "but I just had to tell you the rice pudding was amazing. The best I've ever tasted."

His lips stretched into a grin. "I hope that means you're feeling better?"

"Much better."

"Well, tomorrow I'm making chocolate pudding, updated for more sophisticated tastes. I'd be curious what you think."

"Oh, I'm so sorry I'll miss it. I'm leaving in the morning."

His face crumpled.

"I'd ask for the recipe, but I learned my lesson," I said, forcing a smile.

"Speaking of that, I have something I'd like to say in private. Do you have time for a walk?"

With the way his eyes sparkled, how could I refuse?

Out of habit, I started strolling toward my bungalow and Joseph followed. He didn't speak until we were well away from the main lodge.

"I've decided to give you the recipe for the butterscotch pudding," he announced.

I actually gasped. "You're kidding, right?"

"No, I'm not. I've also decided to tell you why. Even though you might think I'm kind of a creep."

"I can't imagine that I would," I said softly.

"Well, I've been sort of watching you over the past week. The first day at dinner you looked so sad and thin, but you smiled when you ate my food. As the days passed you looked...happier. I thought—well, maybe this will sound stuck-up—but I thought maybe my cooking was helping you feel better."

For a moment I couldn't speak. My chest ached, but sweetly,

as if he'd reached inside and soothed my sore heart. "Actually, I have been going through a rough time, and your food did comfort me. When I tasted your butterscotch pudding last night, I knew I was going to be all right. I wanted to thank you for that, but I didn't think I'd get the chance."

"No, I should thank you. It's nice to make a difference. Sometimes I wonder if anyone even notices," he said.

"I noticed."

"I appreciate that. So, I'm going to give you the recipe, but I'd prefer if you don't let anyone else know about this."

We'd reached my bungalow and I paused before the door. "Of course. Do you mind if we do it in my room so I can take notes?"

The words slipped out before I realized my proposal might have a less innocent interpretation.

But the way Joseph smiled then, well, I suddenly knew everything was going to be all right indeed.

At first we both behaved in a civilized manner. I sat at the desk and wrote the recipe down on the hotel stationery while Joseph stood beside me and dictated. Yet, like the night before, his warmth, his scent, made it hard to concentrate on my task.

When I stood up and thanked him again, he didn't step back. We were standing so close I could have licked him.

"How old are you?" I asked.

"Twenty-six."

"I'm old enough to be your mother."

Joseph just smiled and said, "But you're not."

Then he leaned down and kissed me.

His lips were satin, and his mouth tasted like cream and vanilla and sex, and I wanted to taste him everywhere, just like my fantasy the night before. But it wasn't at all like the fantasy, because Joseph didn't stand passively while I undressed him and sucked his fingers and then his cock. He backed me up to the bed and laid my body over it, as he might arrange the day's special on a plate. And so I was the one who submitted, who closed my eyes and sighed, who shivered when he took my nipple in his mouth and licked and sucked with consummate skill.

I was the one who confessed, in a voice hoarse with need, that I wanted to fuck him so badly, but I didn't have any condoms.

"What's the problem?" he replied with a smile. "After all, we both like to eat."

That's how I found myself with my ass propped on a pillow and Joseph's face buried between my legs. Not surprisingly, he was a master at this kind of dining, too, the ultimate multitasker, flicking my clit with his tongue, while both hands tweaked and pinched my sensitive breasts. He made me so wet, my juices flowed down over my slit, soaking the pillow. But I didn't care; I knew no shame. I came in record time, my thighs shaking, my head thrashing, my hips bucking like a cowboy on a bull. Joseph rode it with me, tonguing me to the finish. I could tell he enjoyed his meal from the glistening grin on his face.

I cleaned my juices from his chin and lips with my tongue and told him it was my turn to eat.

Joseph's cock was medium-length and thick, a perfect mouthful. I ate him like an ice-cream cone, savoring his musk and spice. His groans and sighs told me I hadn't lost my skill. Then I got the naughty idea to ask if he liked a finger up his ass when he was getting a blow job. To my surprise—and delight— he confessed that he'd never done that before, but he was always interested in experimenting with new ingredients.

At last, I could thank him for the pudding in a way he would remember.

Wetting my forefinger in my mouth, I teased him in that

sensitive spot behind his balls, tracing a slippery trail back along his crack to his secret, puckered hole.

"Push open for me," I whispered, easing my fingertip into that tiny, delicate mouth. His hard-on twitched and I pushed farther, gentle in my defloration. I took his cock between my lips and ran the tip of my tongue around the crown. His shaft swelled against my lips, hard as a marble rolling pin, but that made it all the easier to glide up and down, up and down. When his breath quickened, I crooked my finger forward—*come here, come here*—and a few strokes later, my dessert arrived. Tonight's finale was, of course, hot jets of cream splashing against the back of my throat accompanied by a garnish of low, animal moans. I made sure to swirl the chef's special sauce around my mouth before I swallowed. As always, it was exquisite, something only he could make.

Definitely a dish to remember.

And so, although I promised not to share the recipe for the butterscotch pudding, I don't mind passing on the secret for an even sweeter ending to a good meal. I guarantee it will make you very glad you're alive.

Chef Joseph's Creamy Cougar Pudding (serves two generously)
   Ingredients:
   1 brawny, tireless boy chef
   1 fortysomething divorcée with a sweet tooth
   Garnish with:
   1 hotel bed with extra pillows
   A package of condoms purchased from the men's room in the hotel lobby for the next round
   Mix both ingredients together well until they release their natural juices. Repeat as desired.

ABOUT THE
AUTHORS

JACQUELINE APPLEBEE is a writer who breaks down barriers with smut. Her stories have been published in anthologies such as *Best Women's Erotica, Alison's Wonderland* and *Fast Girls.* She can be found online at writing-in-shadows.co.uk.

Born and raised in the San Francisco Bay Area, **OLIVIA ARCHER** now resides in Los Angeles. She isn't your typical California girl who rides the waves of surf, she would rather ride (or write) waves of pleasure.

DEL CARMEN is a sexy Latina from New York City. She is new to erotica and looking forward to exposing more of herself. Visit her at mydelcarmen.blogspot.com.

ELIZABETH COLDWELL lives and writes in London. Her short stories have appeared in numerous anthologies including *Please, Sir; Smooth* and *Orgasmic.* She can be found blogging at The (Really) Naughty Corner, elizabethcoldwell.wordpress. com. She doesn't smoke, but she has no objection to cute men, Dutch or otherwise, who do.

PORTIA DA COSTA pens both romance and women's erotica and is the author of over twenty novels and a hundred-plus short stories. Praised for her vivid, emotional writing, she's best known for her Black Lace titles, but now writes for a variety of publishers, including Harlequin Spice.

JEN CROSS is a writer, performer and writing workshop facilitator. Her writing appears in many anthologies and periodicals, including *Make/Shift, Nobody Passes, Visible: A Femmethology* and *Best Sex Writing 2008*. She tours with the Body Heat Femme Porn Tour and facilitates writing workshops in the Bay Area. For more, visit writingourselveswhole.org.

JUSTINE ELYOT is the author of *On Demand* and *The Business of Pleasure*, as well as having contributed numerous short stories to volumes of erotica and erotic romance. Her work can be found in anthologies from Cleis Press, Black Lace, Xcite Books and Total E-Bound, among others.

KIN FALLON is a writer from England. She likes and wants more love, happiness and pleasure for herself and others. She spends her spare time trying to spread peace and love in the world as best she can.

BRANDY FOX writes poetry, short stories, essays, and novels for both children and adults, but writing erotica has by far been the most fun. She lives in Washington State with her spouse and two boys.

SHANNA GERMAIN has an unending lust for all things shiny and sharp, including knives, nipple clamps and quick wits. You can read more of her work in places like *Best American Erotica, Best Bondage Erotica 2, Best Gay Romance, Best Lesbian Erotica, Bitten, Frenzy* and *Playing With Fire.* Join her other stalkers at shannagermain.com.

K. D. GRACE lives in England with her husband. She is passionate about nature, writing, and sex—not necessarily in that order. She enjoys Chinese martial arts, frightening attempts to learn piano, long distance walking and extreme vegetable gardening. She has published a novel, *The Initiation of Ms. Holly.*

AIMEE HERMAN, a performance poet, currently works as sections editor of erotica for Oysters & Chocolate. She can be read in the anthologies, *Oysters & Chocolate Erotic Stories of Every Flavor, Best Lesbian Love Stories 2010* and *Best Women's Erotica 2010.*

LUCY HUGHES lives by the Gulf of Mexico among the pelicans and palmettos. She is currently in graduate school, and writes fiction when the professors forget to lock the door, allowing her to escape from the lab.

CLANCY NACHT squeezes writing in amongst her job, her husband, and three feral rescue cats. She has written erotic fiction since 2003 but did not delve into professional writing until 2009. Since then she has been published by Cleis Press, Phaze, Ravenous Romance, Noble Romance and Dreamspinner Press.

AIMEE PEARL is the pen name of a kinky bi girl living in that playful paradise known as San Francisco. Her erotic stories—all true-life tales—appear in *Please, Sir: Stories of Female Submission*, *Best Women's Erotica* and *Best Lesbian Erotica*, among other places.

KAYAR SILKENVOICE is a bisexual polyamorous writer living in San Francisco. A postfeminist graduate of one of the Seven Sisters Colleges, she writes to promote sex-positive culture, hosts the weekly Silken On Sex podcast and produces erotic audio recordings. Kayar's passion is sexual exploration. Join her on SilkenOnSex.com.

CHARLOTTE STEIN has published many stories in various erotic anthologies. Her own collection of short stories, *The Things That Make Me Give In*, was named one of the best erotic romances of 2009 by Michelle Buonfiglio. She has novellas and a novel with Ellora's Cave, Total-E-Bound and Xcite, and you can contact her here: themightycharlottestein.blogspot.com.

DONNA GEORGE STOREY is the author of *Amorous Woman*, a very steamy tale of an American woman's love affair with Japan. Her erotic fiction has been published in numerous journals and anthologies including *Clean Sheets, Penthouse, Best Women's Erotica, Best American Erotica* and *X: The Erotic Treasury*. Read more at DonnaGeorgeStorey.com.

AMELIA THORNTON is a very good girl with very bad thoughts, who lives by the English seaside with her collection of school canes, a lot of vintage lingerie and too many shoes. She enjoys baking, hard spankings and writing beautiful naughtiness.

ABOUT
THE EDITOR

RACHEL KRAMER BUSSEL (rachelkramerbussel.com) is a New York–based author, editor and blogger. She has edited over thirty books of erotica, including *Gotta Have It; Best Bondage Erotica 2011; Her Surrender; Obsessed; Orgasmic; Bottoms Up: Spanking Good Stories; Spanked; Naughty Spanking Stories from A to Z 1* and *2; Fast Girls; Smooth; Passion; The Mile High Club; Do Not Disturb; Tasting Him; Tasting Her; Please, Sir; Please, Ma'am; He's on Top; She's on Top; Caught Looking; Hide and Seek; Crossdressing* and *Rubber Sex*. She is series editor of *Best Sex Writing* and winner of six IPPY (Independent Publisher) Awards. Her work has been published in over one hundred anthologies, including *Best American Erotica 2004* and *2006*. She serves as senior editor at *Penthouse Variation*, and is a sex columnist for SexisMagazine.com.

She blogs at lustylady.blogspot.com. Find out more about *Women in Lust* and the contributors at womeninlust.wordpress.com.